"You can never underestimate the power of persistence. Most people break before the case does."
— Lt. Joe Kenda

Elite Desires

Adam McKim

This book is a work of fiction. Names, characters, places, and incidents are the products of the author's imagination or are used fictiously. Any resemblance to actual events, locales, or persons, living or dead, is entirely coincidental.

Chapter 1

Detective Marcus Cole pulled his car into the lot beside Rudy's Diner, a small, weathered establishment whose flickering neon sign spelled "RUDY'S" in uneven blue letters. The relentless rain slicked the pavement, casting distorted reflections of the sign across the alley. Marcus hesitated before stepping out, gripping the steering wheel tightly as the weight of another grim call settled over him.

The echoes of past cases crowded his mind, each one etched with the faces of victims whose stories ended too soon. He could still hear the crackle of distant radios and the murmur of subdued voices in other scenes just like this. The memories blended with the present, a relentless reminder of how little had changed. Every new case threatened to chip away at the resolve he worked so hard to maintain, and tonight was no exception. The thought of yet another life cut short gnawed at him, igniting a restless determination tempered by simmering frustration. Tonight, he promised himself, would be different—somehow. The voices on the radio had been clipped, the details sparse —but the tone told him everything he needed to know. Another scene that would haunt him long after the case closed. But he was determined to find justice, to bring closure to the victim's family, and to make sure this case didn't end up as just another statistic.

As he reached for his hat, Marcus caught sight of another car pulling into the lot. The door opened, and a tall man with a commanding presence stepped out. Chief Gregory Nash—a seasoned veteran with a gruff demeanor that masked a sharp intellect—adjusted his trench coat against the rain. Marcus couldn't help but recall the first time they'd worked together. It had been five years ago, on a case involving a string of arson attacks that terrorized the city. Nash had walked into the precinct like he owned the place, barking orders and demanding answers.

Marcus had initially been put off by the chief's blunt manner, but over the weeks, he'd come to respect Nash's unyielding commitment to justice. They'd cracked the case together, finding the arsonist holed up in an abandoned warehouse, ready to set one final blaze. It was Nash who had spotted the faint glint of a lighter in the darkness and tackled the suspect before the fire could start.

From that moment on, Marcus knew Nash's instincts were razor-sharp, even if his methods were rough around the edges. The chief rarely came to crime scenes himself, which meant he sensed the gravity of this case just as much as Marcus did.

"Detective," Chief Nash greeted, his deep voice cutting through the rain. "Walk me through it."

Marcus nodded, stepping out and bracing against the chill. "Another one," he said grimly. "Female, nineteen. Found in the alley behind the diner."

Together, they approached the narrow alley, where a cluster of officers worked under the harsh glare of portable lights. The alley was a tableau of neglect: discarded boxes, broken pallets, and the pungent smell of wet garbage. Lying face down in the middle of the alley was the body of a young woman, her lifeless form surrounded by the grime and silence of the city. The dim alley lights cast flickering shadows across the scene, illuminating discarded beer cans, crumpled fast-food wrappers, and a single, half-crushed cigarette box lying near her feet. The air reeked of mildew and decay, the oppressive smell of garbage mingling with the sharp tang of rain-soaked concrete.

Nearby officers shifted uneasily, their muted voices tinged with a professional detachment that couldn't completely mask their unease as they discussed the grim discovery. The seasoned officers, with their efficient movements and lack of visible emotion, painted a stark picture of the grim reality they faced daily. Each detail of the surroundings painted a picture of neglect and desolation, a place where life—and now death—seemed all too easily discarded.

Officer Davis met them at the tape, his expression somber. "Chief, Detective. The victim's name is Isabel Vargas. Local. Found about an hour ago by a couple of kids cutting through. They called it in."

Marcus crouched beside the body, his sharp eyes scanning every detail. Isabel's head was tilted slightly, her arms limp at her sides. Her damp clothes—jeans and a lightweight jacket—offered no immediate clues, but the scuff marks on her shoes and the dirt under her chipped fingernails hinted at a struggle.

"She didn't die here," Marcus murmured. "She was brought here."

"That's my read, too," Nash said, his voice heavy. "Anything on her?"

Davis shook his head. "No ID, but her old boss at the diner recognized her. Said she used to work here about six months ago."

Marcus glanced up at the sputtering neon sign above. The diner, with its worn charm, had likely been more than just a job for Isabel. It had been a stepping stone, a symbol of her desire to leave behind small-town life. Now, it was a nexus of questions.

"Why'd she leave the diner?" Marcus asked.

"Boss said she moved to the city for a better-paying job," Davis replied. "Thought she'd moved on to bigger things. Didn't seem like anything was wrong."

Marcus straightened, his eyes narrowing. "And now she's here. Was she reported missing?"

Davis nodded grimly. "Her mom filed a report a few weeks ago. Isabel stopped answering calls. But with her being nineteen and supposedly leaving voluntarily, the case stopped there."

Nash let out a low growl of frustration. "Another one slipped through the cracks," he muttered.

Marcus clenched his jaw. It was a story they'd heard too many times. Young adults were disappearing, and their cases were shelved unless foul play was immediately evident. Now, Isabel Vargas was another name on that list—another failure of a system stretched too thin.

The forensic team worked methodically, photographing and bagging evidence. Marcus watched as Dr. Lorraine Hunt carefully examined Isabel's hands and scraped beneath her nails. The woman's sharp eye for detail had broken more than one case wide open. Marcus silently hoped this would be one of those times.

"Any witnesses?" Nash asked.

"None," Davis said. "The alley doesn't see much traffic, especially in this weather. The kids who found her said she was already here when they arrived."

Marcus scanned the scene, the forensic team's cameras flashing as they documented every angle. The rain-soaked alley told its own story, but the details remained obscured. He stepped closer, his eyes landing on a faint trail of scuff marks leading from the street to where Isabel's body had been placed. The drag marks confirmed what he already suspected: she hadn't walked here herself. As his eyes moved to a nearby dumpster, something caught his attention: a crumpled, dark blue scarf with faint stars woven into it. It was damp and stained, but it didn't belong to Isabel—it hadn't been on her body. Someone else had been here recently.

He bagged it and handed it to Dr. Hunt. "Test this for fibers, DNA, anything useful."

Inside Rudy's Diner, the warmth was a jarring contrast to the scene outside. The patrons, most of whom were regulars, judging by their easy familiarity with Rudy, sat scattered across the checkered tile floor. A man in a worn leather jacket stirred his coffee absently, his eyes fixed on the steam rising from the cup as though it held the answer to an unspoken question. At the far end of the counter, two older women whispered to each other, their voices low but animated as they cast occasional glances toward the windows streaked with rain. A young couple, their hands intertwined on the table, leaned in close, speaking softly —a stark juxtaposition to the grim reality unfolding just outside.

Rudy's radio hummed faintly from the back, the tinny sound of a classic rock station mixing with the clatter of plates and the hiss of the coffee machine. To Marcus, the chatter and routines felt hollow, a fragile veneer of normalcy teetering on the edge of the harsh truth beyond the door. Behind the counter stood Rudy himself, a burly man in his 50s with a salt-and-pepper beard. His expression tightened with worry as Marcus and Nash approached.

"Detective Cole. Chief Nash," Rudy greeted, wiping his hands on his apron. "Damn shame about Isabel. She was a good kid."

"You recognized her right away?" Nash asked.

Rudy nodded. "Hard not to. She worked here for a couple of years. Always on time, polite. She had big plans, though. Said she was gonna make it in the city."

"Did she mention where she was working?" Marcus asked.

"Some recruitment agency," Rudy said. "Elite Opportunities. She left her locker key with me when she quit. Told me I could toss her stuff if I needed the space, but I didn't touch it until a couple of weeks ago."

Rudy reached under the counter and handed Marcus a plastic bag containing a glossy business card. "Figured it might help."

Marcus examined the card. **"Elite Opportunities"** was emblazoned in bold letters above the tagline: *"Unlock Your Future."* Beneath that was a phone number and a website. Something about it felt off—too polished, too generic.

"She never came back here?" Nash asked.

"Not once," Rudy said, his voice tinged with guilt. "Her mom came by a few times asking if I'd heard from her, but I didn't know anything. If I'd known..." He trailed off, his hands trembling.

"You did the right thing holding onto this," Marcus said, pocketing the card. "Sometimes the smallest details crack cases wide open. We'll get to the bottom of this."

Back in the rain, Marcus and Nash stood under the diner's flickering sign. The card in Marcus's pocket felt like a lead, thin but promising. He could almost hear the unspoken urgency in Nash's question before it was even voiced.

"What's your take?" Nash asked.

Marcus's eyes lingered on the alley, his mind piecing together the fragments of Isabel's final moments. "This wasn't random," he said finally. "She didn't die here. Whoever did this wanted her found. The placement, the lack of visible injuries—it's too deliberate."

Nash nodded. "Then let's make sure we find them."

* * *

Marcus returned to the precinct later that night. The business card from Elite Opportunities lay on his desk like a puzzle piece that didn't quite fit. He typed the name into his database search, only to find sparse information. The website listed vague promises of career advancement and limitless potential, but reviews and detailed records were conspicuously absent. A phone number, a P.O. box address, and a handful of generic stock photos were all that backed the agency's existence.

His phone buzzed, jolting him from his thoughts. "Davis," he answered.

"Detective, we ran the number on the card. It's a burner, paid for in cash downtown," Davis reported.

Marcus rubbed his temple. "What about the P.O. box?"

"Registered under the company name," Davis said. "No owner listed."

Marcus sighed, frustration mounting. Every lead seemed to lead nowhere, and yet he couldn't shake the feeling that this agency held the key to Isabel's death. The polished veneer of Elite Opportunities mocked him, a façade of ambition hiding something far darker.

By the time Marcus left the precinct, the rain had slowed to a drizzle. Standing under the streetlights, he thought of Isabel's mother, who had fought to keep her daughter's name from being forgotten. He thought of Rudy, whose guilt weighed heavily despite his efforts to help. Above all, he thought of Isabel herself—her life reduced to a name on a report, her dreams extinguished before they could fully take shape. Clenching his jaw, Marcus resolved that he wouldn't let her case be another unsolved tragedy. The truth was out there, tangled in the lies of Elite Opportunities, and he intended to find it.

Marcus leaned back in his chair. He didn't know where this case would take him, but he knew he wouldn't stop until the answers were his. The rain outside turned into a steady rhythm against the precinct's windows as though marking time against the relentless churn of questions in his mind. Someone knew exactly what had happened to Isabel Vargas, and Marcus vowed he would be the one to find out.

Chapter 2

Marcus paused briefly before Rosa Vargas's door, adjusting his coat against the bitter chill in the air. The rain had subsided into a light drizzle, but the dampness lingered, soaking into his thoughts like the weight of the case pressing down on his shoulders. The persistent moisture mirrored the unease that clung to him, a reminder of how tragedies like this had a way of seeping into every corner of life. Each drop seemed to echo the relentless churn of unanswered questions, blurring the line between the gloom outside and the heaviness in his mind.

When the door finally opened, Marcus met Rosa's eyes, a fragile tension etched into her hollow gaze. She gripped the doorframe, her hand trembling slightly as though bracing herself for whatever he had come to say.

"Mrs. Vargas," Marcus began softly. His tone was measured but heavy with the weight of what he had to deliver. "I'm Detective Marcus Cole. I'm...I'm here about Isabel." He paused, watching her expression flicker between hope and fear. "I'm so sorry to tell you this, but Isabel was found deceased last night."

For a moment, the world seemed too still. Rosa's lips parted as though to protest, but no sound came. Her knees buckled slightly, and she steadied herself against the doorframe. The words hung between them, cruel and irreversible.

"No," she whispered, the word barely audible. Tears welled in her eyes, her face crumpling as the weight of the news settled over her. "No...not my Isabel..."

Marcus stepped forward slightly. "I'm so sorry, Mrs. Vargas," he said again.

This was a woman who had been clinging to hope by the thinnest thread, only for it to snap under the weight of her worst fears. Her eyes carried the haunted look of someone who had replayed every possibility in her mind, each one darker than the last. The slight tremor in her hand, as she gripped the doorframe, spoke of sleepless nights and countless prayers unanswered, leaving her caught in a torturous loop of grief and longing.

After a long moment, Rosa stepped back, motioning for Marcus to enter. Her voice trembled as she spoke. "Come in," she said. "Please."

Marcus nodded, stepping into the apartment. "Thank you, Mrs. Vargas. I know this is incredibly difficult, but I appreciate you taking the time to talk with me."

For a moment, Rosa's lips quivered as though she might speak, but no words came. Instead, she nodded faintly and stepped aside, motioning for him to enter. Marcus crossed the threshold into a modest apartment that carried the faint scent of lavender, struggling to mask the stale air of an aging building. The air felt heavy, as though years of quiet worry had settled into the walls. The faint hum of a refrigerator buzzed from the adjacent kitchen, and the muted creak of old floorboards underfoot added to the stillness. Marcus's eyes moved to a small shelf near the entryway, cluttered with knick-knacks—a ceramic figurine of an angel, a half-burned candle, and a faded postcard of a beach that seemed impossibly far away from this place.

The living room stretched out before him, unassuming yet deeply personal. A small couch with floral upholstery faced a well-worn coffee table, its edges nicked and scuffed from years of use. Mismatched photo frames adorned the walls, each capturing fragments of a life now overshadowed by loss. His gaze was drawn to one frame in particular: a photo of Isabel with a radiant smile, her arms slung around Rosa's shoulders. The optimism in her expression stood in painful contrast to the lifeless body Marcus had seen in the alley the night before. The photo seemed to radiate hope and determination that made the reality of her death feel all the more unjust.

"Please, sit," Rosa said, her voice trembling as she gestured to the couch.

Marcus eased onto the edge of the seat, watching as Rosa lowered herself into an armchair across from him. Her posture was tense, her hands clasped tightly in her lap. The silence between them stretched for a moment, filled only by the faint ticking of a clock on the wall. It was a silence heavy with unspoken fears and unanswered questions, and Marcus could feel the weight of it pressing against his own thoughts.

"I've been trying to get answers for months," Rosa finally said. "The police said there was nothing they could do. They called her a runaway. Just another girl who wanted to leave home."

Her eyes met Marcus's, glistening with unshed tears. "But I knew something was wrong. Isabel wouldn't do that to me. She wouldn't just...disappear without calling."

Marcus nodded, his notepad resting on his knee. "I'm sorry no one listened to you sooner, Mrs. Vargas. I know this is difficult, but I need you to tell me everything you can about Isabel. Anything that might help us understand what happened."

Rosa swallowed hard, her gaze dropping to her clasped hands. "The last time I saw her, she was so happy," she began. "She said she'd gotten a job. A real job in the city. She said it was going to change everything for her—for both of us."

"Did she tell you much about the job?" Marcus asked, leaning forward slightly.

"She said it was with a company called Elite Opportunities," Rosa replied. "She told me it was an office job, something professional. She thought it would pay well enough for her to send money back home to me."

Marcus took down the notes. "And did she seem nervous or hesitant about leaving?"

Rosa shook her head. "No, she was so excited. I told her to be careful, to look into it more, but she kept saying how lucky she was that they'd found her. She said they'd contacted her after seeing her resume online."

Marcus nodded as he continued writing his notes. "Did she leave anything behind? Anything from the company?"

Rosa hesitated, her brow furrowing. "I kept something," she said slowly. "A flyer they gave her. I didn't think much of it at the time, but now..." Her voice cracked, and she stopped. "Let me get it."

As Rosa disappeared down the hallway, Marcus allowed himself a moment to survey the room again. His eyes lingered on Isabel's photograph, her infectious smile radiating the kind of hope and determination he rarely saw in his line of work. It was a stark reminder of the potential she'd had and the life she'd been robbed of. He tightened his jaw, willing himself to focus.

Rosa returned with a crumpled flyer in her trembling hand. She extended it to Marcus, who took it carefully. "This was it," she said, her voice breaking. "She brought it home the day she decided to take the job."

Marcus unfolded the glossy paper, his eyes scanning the bold letters at the top: **Elite Opportunities**. Beneath the name was the same tagline on the business card: *Unlock Your Future*. The rest of the flyer was filled with vague promises: *Exciting career-building roles! Tailored to young professionals!* At the bottom, a phone number and website were printed in fine text.

"She believed in it," Rosa said. "She thought it was her way out of her dead-end job at the diner."

Marcus glanced up at her. "Do you mind if I take this with me? It might help us track down who she was working with."

Rosa nodded quickly. "Take it. Take anything you need."

"Thank you," Marcus said, folding the flyer carefully and tucking it into his coat pocket. "Mrs. Vargas, I know this is painful, but I need to ask: when did you realize something was wrong?"

Rosa's hands gripped the armrests of her chair as she spoke. "When she stopped answering her phone. At first, I thought maybe she was just busy settling into the job. But after a week, I couldn't reach her. Her phone went straight to voicemail. I left so many messages..." Her voice faltered, and she wiped at her eyes. "I went to Rudy's. I thought maybe she'd gone back there, but her boss said she'd already left for the city."

Marcus's pen stilled on his notepad as the weight of Rosa's words settled over him. "Did she ever mention anything strange about the job? Something that didn't sit right with her?"

"No," Rosa said, shaking her head. "She trusted them. She really believed they were going to help her."

Marcus nodded slowly. He'd seen it before: hope turned into a weapon wielded by predators who preyed on vulnerability. Isabel had been no exception.

"Mrs. Vargas," Marcus said gently, "if it's not too much trouble, I'd like to take a look at Isabel's room."

Rosa hesitated, her tired eyes meeting his. For a moment, she seemed uncertain, but then she nodded. "Of course," she said softly. "It's...it's just the way she left it."

Marcus followed Rosa down a narrow hallway lined with faded wallpaper. The faint sound of rain tapping against the window at the end of the hall was a reminder of the dreary world outside. Rosa stopped in front of a door that was slightly ajar. Her hand lingered on the doorknob before she pushed it open.

The room was small but meticulously organized. A twin bed with a simple blue comforter was pushed against one wall, and a desk sat beneath the window, cluttered with notebooks, pens, and framed photos.

Posters of musicians and movies adorned the walls, vibrant against the muted tones of the apartment.

Marcus stepped inside, his gaze sweeping the space. He moved to the desk, where a notebook lay open. The page was filled with lists in neat handwriting: job applications, places to visit, and a section titled Goals. Marcus's chest tightened as he read through the list, each item a window into Isabel's aspirations. They were simple, almost achingly so: Get a good job. Save money to help Mom. Take a trip to the beach. Marcus couldn't shake the thought of how close she had been to achieving them—her drive and optimism evident in every careful stroke of her pen. He felt a swell of frustration at how easily those dreams had been stolen, replaced by tragedy. It was moments like this that reminded him why he'd taken this job: not just to catch criminals but to give voice to the silenced dreams of people like Isabel.

He continued scanning the room, his attention drawn to a small stack of envelopes tied together with twine on a bookshelf. Amid the clutter of utility bills and subscription flyers, one envelope stood out. The return address read: **Elite Opportunities.**

Marcus opened it carefully and unfolded a glossy letter printed on high-quality paper. The layout was sleek, professional, corporate branding with just enough flair to feel personal. At the top, in bold lettering, was the phrase: *"We believe in your potential."*

The letter welcomed the recipient to an exclusive recruitment program, promising access to high-paying career placements, international travel, and mentorship from "industry leaders." But as Marcus read on, a hollow feeling crept into his chest. There were no job titles. No company names. No contact person—just a vague invitation to attend a private intake session.

It was bait. A polished lure meant to entice the ambitious and the vulnerable. He could see how someone like Isabel—young, hungry for a fresh start— might have clung to the promise of something better.

"This helps," Marcus said, setting the letter aside. "It confirms they were actively recruiting her."

Rosa's voice wavered. "She was so smart. But she was still so young. She didn't know how cruel people could be."

"This wasn't her fault," Marcus said firmly. "They preyed on her trust. That's on them."

Rosa nodded faintly, though her tears betrayed the guilt she carried. "I just want justice for her."

"You have my word," Marcus said. "We're going to find out who did this."

As Marcus left the apartment, the image of Isabel's room stayed with him: the photos, the lists, the letter promising a future she'd never see. This wasn't just a case anymore. It was personal.

Chapter 3

Marcus stepped into the precinct, his shoes squeaking faintly on the damp tile floor as he shrugged off his rain-soaked coat. The storm outside had quieted, but the lingering scent of wet asphalt and stale coffee clung to the air. He glanced around at the familiar chaos of the station—phones ringing sporadically, officers hunched over desks typing reports, and the faint buzz of overhead fluorescent lights.

He made his way to his desk, dropping his coat on the back of his chair, setting the recruitment flyer and letter from Elite Opportunities in front of him. His eyes lingered on the glossy paper, the weight of Isabel's death pressing heavily on his chest. He couldn't help but think of her smile in the photos her mother had shown him, so full of hope and ambition, now reduced to a tragic memory. A wave of cold anger simmered beneath his professional exterior. But more than anger, there was a determination, a resolve to not let Isabel's memory fade into the shadows. Every lead felt like a lifeline—not just to uncover the truth but to honor the future Isabel had been robbed of.

Her body in that cold, rain-slicked alley was a sight he wouldn't soon forget. But it wasn't just the violence of her death that haunted him—it was the unanswered questions. Who had lured her into the trap? How many more had fallen victim? Marcus's fingers tapped against the edge of his desk, his mind racing through possibilities. Each question brought another layer of frustration, the pieces of a puzzle scattered and yet tauntingly close.

With a sigh, Marcus logged into the precinct's missing persons database. The system's outdated interface loaded sluggishly, the search bar blinking at him as if to mock his impatience. He typed Isabel's name, pulling up her case file. The sparse details stared back at him: 19 years old, presumed runaway, last seen leaving her home six months ago. No signs of foul play were reported.

Marcus clenched his jaw as he read through the dismissive notes. Rosa Vargas's pleas for help had been waved off, reduced to bureaucratic indifference hidden behind cold, clinical language. It was the kind of systemic failure he'd seen too many times before—cases where a lack of urgency condemned victims to the shadows. He felt a surge of anger at how easily Isabel's life had been dismissed as if she were just another statistic in an endless pile of unresolved files. This wasn't just negligence; it was complicity in allowing predators to thrive.

"You deserved better," Marcus muttered under his breath, shaking his head.

Clearing Isabel's file from the screen, Marcus entered a new search. This time, he typed in Elite Opportunities, a seemingly reputable company that had turned into a nightmare for too many families. He adjusted the filters, narrowing the results to missing persons cases over the last two years and focusing on women aged 18 to 25. As the system churned, Marcus leaned back, his fingers tapping against the desk. When the results finally appeared, his stomach sank.

Five other names. Five young women. All disturbingly similar.

Marcus opened the first file, his eyes scanning the text. Sofia Ramirez, 20 years old, was last seen at a bus station en route to an interview arranged by Elite Opportunities. Her photo stared back at him: a young woman with soft brown eyes, her wavy black hair falling past her shoulders. Her shy smile hinted at someone who'd been hesitant to take risks but had decided to step outside her comfort zone. Missing for eight months.

The following case involved Hannah Lee, a 19-year-old who had left her job at a convenience store after receiving an interview invitation. A business card for Elite Opportunities was found in her apartment. Her photo showed a girl with striking almond-shaped eyes framed by jet-black bangs, her look carrying a subtle determination that belied her youthful demeanor. Missing for five months.

Marcus continued through the files, noting the haunting similarities. Natalie Brewer, 22, had been last seen attending a job fair where Elite Opportunities had set up a booth. Her bright green eyes sparkled in the photo, and her shoulder-length auburn hair framed her face in soft waves. She looked confident, someone who had believed she was finally taking control of her future. Missing for nine months.

Kara Mitchell, 18, was last seen boarding a train to meet a recruiter. Her photo was striking: blonde curls cascading over her shoulders, her piercing blue eyes giving her a model-like appearance. Yet there was a subtle uncertainty in her expression, a vulnerability beneath the surface. Missing for seven months.

Finally, there was Alexis Nguyen, 21, who had left her university dormitory after receiving a flyer similar to the one Isabel had shown her mother. Alexis had a delicate beauty—smooth, honey-toned skin, long, sleek black hair, and warm brown eyes. Her photo radiated optimism, as if she genuinely believed she was on the cusp of something great. Missing for six months.

As Marcus jotted down notes, a chilling pattern emerged. All the women were beautiful in their own unique ways—attractive, youthful, and ambitious. They'd each been lured by the same promises and had trusted the same glossy façade. And now, they were all gone.

He printed out the files and spread them across his desk, each one a stark reminder of lives that had been interrupted. The photos stared back at him, the women's smiles now haunting in hindsight. Isabel's case wasn't an anomaly—it was part of something larger, a calculated operation that thrived on deception and cruelty. Marcus's pen hovered over his notepad as he scribbled connections, the weight of each name pulling him further into a growing web of despair.

"Hey, Cole," a voice interrupted his thoughts. "You look like you're staring at a murder board."

Marcus glanced up to see Detective Dana Riggs, a seasoned veteran with a sharp mind and no-nonsense demeanor, leaning against the edge of his desk, her arms crossed. She was one of the few people Marcus trusted implicitly, and her presence always brought a sense of reassurance. She raised an eyebrow at the spread of files, clearly intrigued.

"Something like that," Marcus replied, gesturing for her to take a look.

Dana stepped closer, her keen eyes scanning the documents. She picked up the flyer for Elite Opportunities, her brow furrowing as she read it. "This looks slick. Too slick for the kind of trouble you're sniffing out. What is this, a recruitment scam?"

"That's the question," Marcus said. "Six women, including Isabel Vargas. All of them disappeared in the last year. All of them are connected to this company."

Dana let out a low whistle, setting the flyer back down on the table. "That's not a coincidence. This is organized."

Marcus nodded. "It's too clean. No real address, no reviews, no verifiable employees. Just P.O. boxes and burner phones."

Dana crossed her arms, her expression darkening. "I've heard whispers about something like this. It's not just a scam—it's a pipeline." She paused, her eyes narrowing as if drawing on fragments of stories she'd pieced together over the years. "These operations are sophisticated. They target the vulnerable—runaways, immigrants, and anyone desperate for a way out. The victims are groomed, isolated, and then swallowed up into a network that's nearly impossible to trace."

"A pipeline for what?" Marcus asked.

"Trafficking," Dana said bluntly. "There's been talk for years about a network operating in the region. They use fronts like this to lure people in. Once they've got their victims isolated, they disappear."

Marcus leaned back in his chair, Dana's words settling heavily in his mind. If Elite Opportunities was tied to trafficking, then Isabel's death was just one piece of a much larger and more insidious puzzle. His gaze fell back to the photographs spread across his desk—the women's faces staring at him with an unnerving naivety etched into their expressions. Each one had stepped into a trap, believing they were reaching for something better. Instead, they had vanished without a trace.

"How do they stay invisible for so long?" Marcus asked, his voice low. "Six women in a year, all connected to the same company, and no one notices?"

Dana exhaled sharply, shaking her head. "They're smart. They've built layers of protection. They use recruiters who act as buffers so the people at the top never get their hands dirty. When someone gets suspicious, they cut ties and vanish before anyone can follow the trail. They've perfected the art of disappearing."

Marcus frowned, rubbing his temples. "What about the recruiters? Someone has to be working these cases on the ground."

"They're usually small-timers," Dana said. "People who don't even realize what they're part of—or if they do, they're too scared to talk. These networks don't just disappear victims, Marcus. They make sure anyone who crosses them stays quiet."

The room seemed to grow colder as Marcus processed her words. "So what you're saying is, they're untouchable."

"Not untouchable," Dana corrected. "But damn close. If you're pursuing these individuals, you'll need leverage. Something big enough to crack the shell."

Marcus glanced at the bulletin board behind him, his desk now a chaotic map of connections, names, and dates. "And how the hell do I get that leverage?"

Dana hesitated, then crossed her arms. "There might be a way. It's not conventional, but it's worth a shot."

Marcus turned to her, his interest piqued. "What are you talking about?"

"There's a journalist—Elaine Monroe," Dana said. "She's been poking around cases like these for months. She's got a knack for finding cracks in even the tightest operations. I've seen her dig up dirt on people who thought they were untouchable, from shady politicians to organized crime rings. She's relentless, but that's also what makes her dangerous. She'll go to places we can't and talk to people who wouldn't trust a badge. The risk is that once she gets involved, you lose control of the narrative. But if anyone could get leads on Elite Opportunities, it's her."

Marcus's lips tightened. Journalists were unpredictable. They could be helpful, but they could also complicate things, dragging investigations into the spotlight before they were ready. "What does she know?"

"Enough to make people nervous," Dana said. "She's been following the trafficking news for a while now. If she's sniffing around Elite Opportunities, it may be time for us to reach out to her before she gets too deep."

Marcus tapped his pen against his desk, weighing the options. "Journalists don't do anything out of the kindness of their hearts. What does she want?"

"Justice, as far as I can tell," Dana said with a faint smirk. "But she'll want to work the story, no doubt about it. She's not the type to sit back while you run the show."

"That's exactly what worries me," Marcus muttered. "The last thing I need is some reporter blowing this case wide open before we're ready."

"I get it," Dana said. "But think about it, Marcus. If she has something solid, it could be the edge you're looking for. You need someone who knows how these people operate—and she might already have answers you don't."

Marcus leaned forward, resting his elbows on his desk. He hated the idea of bringing the media into an active investigation, but he couldn't deny the possibility that Monroe might have information he couldn't afford to ignore.

"Do you trust her?" Marcus asked finally.

Dana shrugged. "I trust her to stick her nose where it doesn't belong. But she's not reckless."

Marcus sighed. "Fine. Set it up."

Dana smirked. "You're going to regret this."

"Probably," Marcus said, already bracing himself for the meeting. "But if she has what we need, I'll deal with it."

* * *

The precinct was quieter now, the hum of activity fading as the night shift settled in. Marcus stared at the faces on the bulletin board, each one a reminder of what was at stake. Sofia, Hannah, Natalie, Kara, Alexis—and Isabel. Six women, all connected by the same promises, the same lies. And those were just the ones he knew about. How many more were out there, their stories untold, their faces missing from the database?

Marcus's phone buzzed, breaking the silence. He glanced at the screen and saw a message from Dana:

"Monroe wants to meet tomorrow. I told her you'd reach out."

He set the phone down and stood, stretching his stiff muscles before gathering the files from his desk. Tomorrow, he'd meet with Monroe. With any luck, she'd have the answers he needed to break the case wide open. But he knew it wouldn't be that easy. If he was going to take down Elite Opportunities, he'd need more than information. He'd need a plan—and the determination to see it through.

As he left the precinct, the storm outside had finally passed. But Marcus knew the real storm was just about to begin.

Chapter 4

Marcus pushed open the door to the bustling coffee shop, his sharp eyes scanning the crowded room. Apprehension churned in his gut, though his expression remained as composed as ever. Meetings like this weren't unusual in his line of work, but the stakes felt higher today. Conversations buzzed over the clinking of mugs and dishes, providing a perfect cover for a clandestine meeting. He preferred quieter places for discussions like this, but he understood the value of blending in. Besides, anonymity in plain sight had its advantages—especially when dealing with someone as unpredictable as a journalist.

In the far corner, Elaine Monroe was waiting. Her posture was poised and confident, as though she had been in control of this meeting long before Marcus arrived. She sat with her back straight, one hand resting lightly on the edge of a thick folder while the other occasionally adjusted her coffee mug. Her hazel eyes scanned the room with a keen, calculating intensity as if she were cataloging every detail.

"Detective Cole," she greeted, standing and extending her hand.

"Ms. Monroe," Marcus replied, his handshake firm but brisk.

Monroe smiled. "You can just call me Elaine."

Sliding into the seat across from her, he didn't waste time on pleasantries. "Let's get one thing straight. I'm here because you may be of value to our investigation, not because I'm looking for a journalist to work with."

Elaine raised an eyebrow, unfazed by his directness. "Fair enough," she said as she sat back down. "But you're here, which tells me you already think this is worth your time."

Marcus's expression remained unreadable as he gestured toward the folder on the table. "That's it?"

"Months of work," Elaine replied, sliding it across to him. "Everything I've uncovered about Elite Opportunities and the people behind it."

"So you already know about it," Marcus said as he picked up the folder.

Elaine nodded. "I got a business card from a victim's mother."

Marcus flipped open the folder, his sharp gaze scanning the contents with the meticulousness of someone searching for hidden meaning. His eyes lingered on each page, his brow furrowing deeper as he processed the information.

A photograph of a young woman at a gala caught his attention. Her smile was forced, her body language rigid, as though she were aware of the danger lurking beneath the glamorous setting. Marcus's stomach churned.

"Charity galas?" Marcus muttered, his tone skeptical. "That's their hunting ground?"

"Exactly," Elaine said. "These aren't random disappearances, Detective. They target young women who stand out—attractive, ambitious, often vulnerable. They lure them in with promises of opportunity, isolate them from their support systems, and then they disappear."

Marcus clenched his jaw, flipping to another page. A web of transactions linked accounts in Panama, the Cayman Islands, and Switzerland. Monroe's annotations detailed the movement of the money, but the connections were tenuous.

"Money laundering," Marcus said, his tone flat.

"Precisely," Elaine confirmed. "Elite Opportunities is just the tip of the iceberg. The real money flows through these accounts, hidden behind layers of legitimate businesses and shell corporations. It's a carefully orchestrated operation."

Closing the folder, Marcus leaned back in his chair. "You've done your homework, I'll give you that. But this?" He tapped the folder. "This isn't enough to bring them down. You've got breadcrumbs but no direct line to the people running the show."

Elaine's expression hardened, but a flicker of something more personal crossed her face. "When I started digging into Elite Opportunities, I thought it was just another story—one more corruption lead. But then I started talking to families. Mothers who'd been begging for answers. Sisters who still keep their phones on at night in case someone calls. You can't walk away from that. Not when you know what's happening to these girls."

She straightened slightly, regaining her edge. "That's why I'm not just handing you breadcrumbs. I'm trying to help you blow this open."

Marcus's gaze sharpened. "And how do you suggest I do that?"

Elaine leaned forward, her voice steady but intense. "You go undercover."

Marcus stared at her, disbelief flashing across his face. "Undercover. As what?"

"As a client," she said simply. "Someone looking to buy what they're selling."

Her words hung heavy in the air. Marcus shook his head. "These people don't just take your word for it. They'll vet me and dig into my background. If they find one thing that doesn't add up—I'm dead. You think they'll just let it go? These aren't gang bangers with something to prove. These people erase threats. And if they don't come after me, they'll go after anyone I've worked with. My team, my sources. Hell, even you."

He paused briefly, then leaned forward. "I've worn wires before. Posed as buyers, dealers, smugglers—but this is different. Traffickers don't just kill you. They vanish you. And if this goes sideways, no one will even know where to start looking."

"They won't," Elaine interrupted. "Your cover will be airtight. Financials, business dealings, and even references. These people value secrecy, and they're not going to dig deeper unless you give them a reason to."

"This is different," Marcus said sharply.

Elaine's composed demeanor cracked, a flash of frustration breaking through. "And how many Isabels will you have to bury while you wait for the perfect plan?" she snapped.

The words sliced through Marcus like a blade. For a moment, he couldn't speak; his breath caught in his chest. Isabel's face flashed in his mind, followed by the others—smiling photos now haunting reminders of lives destroyed. A knot of guilt and anger tightened in his stomach, fueling a sharp resolve born from his lingering frustration. He glanced at Elaine, her eyes ablaze with conviction, and though her tone was cutting, he couldn't deny the truth behind her words. She had struck a nerve, and the weight of inaction suddenly felt unbearable.

Elaine leaned closer, her hazel eyes blazing. "Every day we hesitate, more women vanish. If you want to play it safe, fine—but understand what that costs. These people don't stop. They don't slow down. And the longer we wait, the harder it'll be to stop them."

Marcus shook his head. "Even if I wanted to go undercover, it's not that simple. These people don't just let strangers into their world. I'd need a damn good reason to be there."

Elaine's posture shifted slightly, a flicker of satisfaction crossing her face. "That's why I wanted to tell you about Jenna Clarke."

Marcus frowned. "Jenna Clarke? The name sounds familiar."

"She's a survivor," she explained. "She escaped the network six months ago."

Recognition flickered in his eyes. "Wait—Jenna Clarke? Wasn't she the one who was all over the news when she escaped? Then suddenly she was just gone."

Elaine nodded. "From what I've gathered, she's under federal protection."

Marcus's eyes narrowed. "And how the hell did you get that information?"

"I didn't at first," she admitted. "She contacted me a few months ago under a fake name. It took time, but I eventually pieced it together. She was scared, paranoid —and then she vanished. That's when I started digging harder."

Marcus's skepticism flared. "If she's in witness protection, that means she's already talked to law enforcement. Why hasn't anything actionable come from her testimony?"

"Maybe she didn't say much," Elaine said. "Maybe she shuts down when they push. Jenna's terrified—and for good reason. The traffickers make sure their victims understand the consequences of talking."

"And you think I'll have better luck?" Marcus asked, his tone skeptical.

"She's working with a trauma specialist," Elaine continued. "Dr. Camille Ford."

Marcus raised an eyebrow. "How do you know that?"

"She mentioned her once, Dr. Ford. She said she was the only one she could somewhat trust. I looked her up. She's low-profile but respected. A trauma specialist who's consulted with law enforcement before. If anyone can help you get through to Jenna, it's her."

Marcus leaned back, processing the information. He wasn't a stranger to working with trauma victims, but Jenna's situation sounded especially fragile. Gaining her trust would take time and care, and even then, there were no guarantees. The idea of involving her left a sour taste in his mouth, but he couldn't ignore the potential.

"What makes you so sure she'll talk to me?" he asked.

"I'm not sure," Elaine admitted. "But I think she wants to talk. Deep down, she wants justice, not just for herself, but for every other woman who didn't make it out. She just doesn't know how to take that first step."

Marcus exhaled sharply, running a hand over his face. The prospect of involving Jenna left him uneasy, but Elaine wasn't wrong. If Jenna could provide even one lead—a name, a location, anything—it could be the key to infiltrating the operation.

"All right," Marcus said finally. "I'll talk to Dr. Ford. If she thinks Jenna's ready, I'll approach her. But if there's even a hint that this will do more harm than good, I'm pulling the plug."

"Agreed," Elaine said quickly. "But if Jenna can give you the connection you need, it'll change everything."

Marcus nodded. "Let's say we get a lead. Any ideas on how we go about this cover you're suggesting?"

Elaine leaned forward, her tone focused. "Here's what I'm thinking for your cover: a mid-level entrepreneur. Someone who looks successful, comfortable, but not flashy enough to raise eyebrows. I've seen this work before. A few years back, there was a sting operation targeting a counterfeit art ring. They used a similar setup—a detective posing as an investor with a niche interest in high-value art. By blending into their world and building trust through carefully planned interactions, he successfully infiltrated the inner circle. If we mirror that approach here, there's a strong chance you'll be able to do the same."

"You'll need to start small," She continued. "Attend the right events, make the right connections. They don't just hand out invitations to their world—you'll have to earn their trust."

Marcus frowned. "And what happens when they dig into my cover?"

"They won't," she said. "Your cover will be airtight. You just leave that to me."

Marcus shook his head, tension creeping into his voice. "I don't think Chief Nash is going to go along with this. He'll shut it down before it even—"

"Then don't tell him," Elaine interrupted. "You said it yourself—these people vanish threats. Every layer of bureaucracy we go through is another chance for them to get tipped off. You want to play by the rules, fine. But while you're doing that, more girls disappear. Think about that."

Marcus nodded slowly, though his mind continued to run through the risks. The plan required precision, and even the slightest misstep could blow the entire operation. But Elaine was right about one thing—standing on the outside wasn't going to stop this.

"And if I do get in?" Marcus asked. "What's the endgame?"

"You gather evidence," Elaine said. "Names, transactions, locations—anything we can use to bring the operation down. And when the time is right, you call for backup, and we expose everything."

Marcus exhaled sharply, rubbing the back of his neck. "You make it sound simple."

"It's not," Elaine admitted. "But it's the only way to stop them."

As Marcus stood to leave, the folder tucked under his arm, Elaine's voice stopped him. "One last thing."

He turned, his expression cautious.

"This isn't just about taking down a network," she said. "It's about giving the victims—like Jenna—the justice they deserve. Don't lose sight of that."

Marcus nodded, her words lingering as he stepped outside into the cool evening air. He stood for a moment, staring down at the folder in his hands. The risks were monumental, but so were the stakes. For

Isabel. For Jenna. For every woman caught in the same web of lies. This was a path he couldn't turn back from.

Chapter 5

The phone buzzed violently on the nightstand, cutting through the fog of a restless night. Marcus jolted awake, groaning as he reached for it, eyes narrowing against the screen's glow. Rosa Vargas. He sat up straight, adrenaline kicking in. Calls at this hour were never good.

"Rosa?" he answered.

"Detective," she said quickly. Her voice was soft, tired, but too steady for someone calling in a panic. "I'm sorry for the hour. I couldn't sleep."

Marcus rubbed his eyes, trying to bring his thoughts into focus. "That's alright. What's going on?"

"I just..." She hesitated, as though debating whether to continue. "I keep thinking about Isabel. About how she ended up in that alley. I keep wondering if it was random or if someone targeted her."

Marcus leaned back against the headboard. "We're still looking into it. I promise you, we're not letting anything slide."

"I know you're doing everything you can," she said, almost too quickly. "I was just wondering...have there been other girls? Since Isabel, I mean. Other disappearances?"

Marcus hesitated. "That's not something I can really get into."

"Of course," Rosa said. Another pause. "But there have been others, haven't there?"

Marcus frowned. "We're investigating all leads."

Rosa let out a shaky breath. "I'm sorry. I'm probably grasping at straws. It just feels like the only thing I can do is try to understand what happened. Otherwise, it keeps playing in my head, over and over."

"I get it," Marcus said gently. "You're not grasping. You're trying to make sense of something that doesn't make sense. That's normal."

There was another silence. Then: "Do you think Isabel ever had a chance?"

The question landed like a stone. Marcus didn't answer right away.

"We don't know how long she was held," he said carefully. "But we're looking into everyone she might've crossed paths with—anyone who might've seen something. I promise you, Rosa, we're not giving up."

"Okay," she said quietly. "Thank you. I'm sorry again for waking you."

"It's alright," he said. "Try to get some rest if you can."

"I'll try," she murmured, and then the line went dead.

Marcus stared at the screen in the dark. The conversation hadn't been emotional, exactly. If anything, it felt...measured. Her voice had trembled a little, but the questions came a bit too prepared, a bit too focused. Still, he shook the thought away. Grief came in all shapes. Some people shut down. Others became obsessed. And some just needed to feel like they were part of the search.

He lay back down, but sleep didn't return.

* * *

The next morning, Marcus arrived at the precinct early, the weight of Rosa's call still lingering in his mind. The sky outside was a dull smear of gray, as if the city itself hadn't quite woken up yet. He found Dana already at her desk, sorting through overnight reports with a mug of black coffee in hand.

"You look like hell," she said, not unkindly.

"Didn't sleep much," Marcus replied, dropping into the chair across from her. "Got a call from Rosa Vargas last night."

Dana raised an eyebrow. "What happened?"

"Nothing urgent," he said. "She said she couldn't sleep. Wanted to ask about Isabel. Then she started asking if there were other missing girls, if we'd found any connections."

Dana sipped her coffee, then lowered the mug slowly. "That's...a little specific."

"Yeah," Marcus said. "I thought so too. But she didn't push. Just asked once or twice. Sounded more sad than anything."

"You think she's fishing for something?" Dana asked.

Marcus thought for a moment, then replied, "I think she's a mother who lost her daughter in the worst possible way and is trying to find some kind of explanation. Still, it wouldn't hurt to keep an eye on her. If the traffickers knew Isabel, there's a chance Rosa's being watched too."

Dana gave a short nod. "I'll get someone on it."

Marcus hesitated, then added, "I met with Elaine Monroe yesterday."

Dana nodded. "Good. I figured you'd follow up."

"She gave me something worth chasing," Marcus said. "Told me about a survivor—Jenna Clarke. She's in some kind of federal protection, but she was in contact with Elaine for a while. Mentioned a trauma specialist she trusted—Dr. Camille Ford."

Dana's eyebrows lifted. "Dr. Ford? I've heard of her. She doesn't advertise, but she has done advisory work with PDs and a few federal task forces. You want to talk to her?"

Marcus nodded. "I want to find out if she thinks Jenna might be ready to talk. Not to pressure her, just...see if there's a way in."

Dana hesitated, "We should probably run this through Nash. If Jenna's federally protected, we can't just go sniffing around—especially not if there's a protective detail involved."

Marcus shook his head. "Not yet. I want to keep this quiet. I'm not asking you to track Jenna down—I just want a conversation with Dr. Ford. Nothing official. Just see if she's willing to meet, talk off the record."

Dana frowned. "Even off the record, this is sticky."

"I know," Marcus said. "But if we loop Nash in too soon, it gets buried in red tape, or worse, flagged in some database that tips the wrong people off. We've already seen what happens before when word leaks."

Dana looked at him for a long moment, then gave a short nod. "Alright. I'll reach out discreetly. No promises."

"That's all I'm asking," Marcus said. "If Ford says no, we drop it. But if she's open to talking...it could be the first real lead we've had."

* * *

That evening, Marcus parked a few houses down from Rosa's home, his unmarked car nestled beneath the shadow of a broad oak. A patrol cruiser sat idle at the corner, lights off but engine running, manned by two uniformed officers taking turns keeping watch. The quiet hum of the neighborhood gave no indication that anything was wrong. Porch lights flickered on and off as timers kicked in. A dog barked somewhere down the street, then fell silent.

From his vantage point, Marcus could see the glow of a lamp in Rosa's living room, curtains drawn tight. No movement. No shadows passing by the window. Just stillness. She hadn't called again. He hadn't expected her to.

He tightened his grip on the steering wheel, staring at the silent house. Her questions still nagged at him— not because they were alarming, but because they were almost too casual. She hadn't asked anything a grieving mother couldn't have. But there was a thread of calculation beneath the surface, one he couldn't quite name. He shook the thought off.

He thought of Isabel, then Sofia, Hannah, Kara, and Alexis. All the names written on the whiteboard in the conference room. The lives behind them. The silence that followed each one. Marcus lingered a moment longer, eyes fixed on Rosa's house.

His phone buzzed on the console. He glanced at the screen. Dana.

Marcus answered, his voice low. "Yeah," he said.

"She's in," Dana said. "Dr. Ford. Just got off the phone with her. She's willing to meet."

Marcus sat forward slightly. "When?" he asked.

"Tomorrow afternoon," Dana replied. "She didn't want to make promises about Jenna. Just said she's open to a conversation and wants to get a read on you first."

"Text me the time and place," Marcus said.

"I will," Dana replied. "And Marcus? Be careful."

"Yeah," Marcus said. "Always."

Dana ended the call, and the line went dead. Marcus leaned back, started the engine, and eased the car into gear. As he pulled away from the shoulder and drove past the house, he caught a glimpse of the curtain shifting—just enough to reveal Rosa watching from the window.

Chapter 6

Marcus parked his car in front of the unassuming safe house, his hands gripping the steering wheel as he prepared himself. The case had taken its toll, and he was acutely aware of how delicate this meeting would be. The house blended seamlessly into the suburban street, its appearance deliberately ordinary. Marcus stepped out, adjusting his tie and bracing himself for what was likely to be a difficult encounter. He approached the door and knocked twice. After a moment, it opened to reveal a woman in plain clothes who gave him a brief nod and stepped aside to let him in without a word.

"Detective Cole," she greeted softly. "Thank you for keeping this off the books. I understand the risks you're taking just being here."

Marcus nodded. "I appreciate you agreeing to meet, Dr. Ford. I didn't want to go through channels and risk alerting the wrong people."

"I understand," Dr. Ford said. "Let's get started. Before you meet Jenna, there's something you need to know."

Marcus's brow furrowed. "What is it?"

Dr. Ford's voice lowered, her tone tinged with sadness. "Her escape came at a cost. She was caught during the attempt—her throat was cut, and she was left for dead. Miraculously, her attacker was in a hurry, and the wound wasn't deep enough to kill her. Still, the recovery was grueling. It left a scar—both physical and emotional. Please be mindful of that during your conversation. She's extremely sensitive about it."

Marcus's stomach twisted at the thought. "Understood. Thank you for telling me."

Dr. Ford nodded. "She's been through unimaginable trauma, but she's stronger than she realizes. Just go easy on her."

Marcus followed Dr. Ford into the living room, the air heavy with quiet tension. The space was a carefully curated sanctuary—warm, neutral, and safe. Jenna sat on the couch, her body stiff and her hands clutching the sleeves of her oversized sweater. Her long hair fell around her face, partially obscuring her wide, haunted eyes. She glanced up briefly as Marcus entered, then quickly looked away.

Dr. Ford sat beside her, an anchor of calm in the storm of Jenna's fragile state. She gave Marcus a small, welcoming smile but kept her focus on Jenna.

Marcus offered a gentle nod and took a seat across from them. "Jenna, it's good to see you," he said. "I know this isn't easy, but I appreciate you taking the time to meet with me."

Jenna's hands fidgeted in her lap, her fingers gripping the fabric of her sweater as if it were her only lifeline. "I…I don't know what to say," she whispered.

"That's okay," Dr. Ford said, her voice warm and reassuring. "You don't have to say anything you're not ready to. Just take your time."

Marcus leaned forward slightly, keeping his posture relaxed. "Jenna, I'm here to listen. Whatever you feel comfortable sharing—it could help us understand what you've been through and how we can stop the people who hurt you."

Jenna's shoulders hunched slightly, her gaze fixed on the floor. "They said…they said no one could stop them," she murmured. "That no one cared."

Her words hit Marcus like a punch to the gut. He exchanged a brief glance with Dr. Ford, who gave a subtle nod, urging him to continue.

"That's not true, Jenna," Marcus said firmly. "You're here because you survived, and we care deeply about what happens to you. The people who told you those things were lying. They wanted to keep you afraid. But you don't have to be afraid anymore."

Jenna's fingers stilled for a moment before resuming their nervous movement. "They…they took everything," she said haltingly. "Our names. Our clothes. Our…our hope. They made us…they made us feel like nothing."

Marcus's chest tightened, but he kept his expression calm. "How did they do that, Jenna?"

Her voice trembled as she spoke, the words spilling out in fragmented pieces. "They told us we didn't matter. That we were just…property. They controlled everything—what we ate, when we slept, when we… worked."

She stopped abruptly, her breathing quickening. Dr. Ford immediately stepped in, guiding her through a grounding exercise. "Breathe with me, Jenna," she said softly, inhaling and exhaling in a slow, deliberate rhythm. "In through your nose, out through your mouth. That's it."

Marcus waited, his hands resting on his knees as he observed the interaction. Jenna followed Dr. Ford's lead, her breathing gradually evening out. The panic in her eyes subsided, replaced by a lingering sadness.

"You're safe now, Jenna," Dr. Ford reminded her gently. "No one can hurt you here."

Jenna nodded faintly, though her hands still trembled. "It…it doesn't feel real," she admitted. "Like…like they'll come back for me."

"They won't," Marcus said firmly. "We won't let that happen."

Jenna glanced up at him briefly, her eyes searching his face for reassurance. "Do you really think you can stop them?"

Marcus met her gaze, his voice steady. "Yes, I do. But I can't do it alone. That's why your bravery is so important, Jenna. What you've been through—it's horrific, but your story can help us stop this from happening to anyone else."

Jenna hesitated, her fingers tightening around the fabric of her sweater. "There was…a man," she said quietly. "He was in charge. He told us what to do."

Marcus leaned forward slightly, his attention sharpening. "Do you remember his name?"

Jenna shook her head. "No…but he was…mean. He looked at us like we were nothing. Like…like we were already dead."

The room fell silent, the weight of her words hanging heavily in the air. Dr. Ford reached over and gave Jenna's shoulder a gentle squeeze. "You're doing so well, Jenna. Thank you for sharing that."

Jenna's lips pressed into a thin line, her eyes flickering toward Marcus. "Is… is it really going to help?" she asked hesitantly.

Marcus nodded, his voice filled with quiet conviction. "Yes, Jenna. Every detail you share brings us closer to stopping them."

The tension in the room was palpable as Jenna hesitated, her gaze dropping to the floor. Dr. Ford, ever patient, gave her another reassuring squeeze on the shoulder, her calm voice bridging the silence.

"You've done incredibly well today, Jenna," Dr. Ford said softly. "Sharing what you've been through takes an immense amount of strength."

Jenna nodded faintly, her hands still gripping her sweater. "I just… I want them to pay," she whispered. "For what they did to all of us."

Marcus leaned forward, resting his forearms on his knees. "We're working on that, Jenna. And what you've shared today is a critical step. However, I want to ensure we're doing everything possible to support you."

Dr. Ford reached out and gently took Jenna's hands. "Jenna, I want to introduce you to someone else," she said.

Jenna's brow furrowed, her shoulders tensing. "Someone else?" she echoed nervously.

"Yes," Dr Ford replied. "Jenna, I've been working with another survivor. Her name is Maya Lopez. She's further along in her recovery and has expressed a desire to help others who have been through what she has. I believe that hearing her story—and perhaps sharing some of your own—could be empowering for both of you."

Jenna's gaze darted to Marcus, then back to Dr. Ford. "I…I don't know if I can do that."

"And that's okay," Dr. Ford assured her. "There's no pressure. It's just an option, and we'll move at your pace. But I do believe Maya's perspective could help you, especially as you work through these memories."

Marcus nodded, backing up Dr. Ford's suggestion. "Maya might also be able to fill in some gaps. If she remembers something similar to what you've experienced, it could help us piece together more of the operation."

Jenna's hands fidgeted again, her uncertainty clear. "What if she thinks I'm…weak?" she asked in a small voice.

Dr. Ford's expression softened. "She won't. Maya understands better than anyone how much courage it takes to survive. She's not here to judge you, Jenna. She's here to stand with you."

For a long moment, Jenna didn't speak. Then, with a shaky breath, she nodded. "Okay…I'll try."

Dr. Ford smiled warmly. "That's all we can ask. Thank you, Jenna."

Dr. Ford stepped out of the room and returned moments later with Maya Lopez. She paused in the doorway, offering Jenna a reassuring look before speaking.

"Jenna," Dr. Ford said gently, "before Maya joins us, I want you to know something important. In light of the new cases of missing girls, Maya has agreed to come back into witness protection for her safety. She'll be staying here with you at the safe house for as long as you are comfortable with it. You're not alone."

Jenna's eyes widened slightly.

Dr. Ford continued, her voice calm. "I'll be here with you both, and nothing about this arrangement changes unless you're ready. Maya's presence is meant to support, not overwhelm."

Jenna's wide eyes flicked toward Maya as she entered, her posture stiffening with apprehension.

"Hi, Jenna," Maya said, her tone surprisingly gentle as she sat down beside her. "Dr. Ford told me a bit about you. I know how hard it is to talk about this stuff, so…thanks for letting me join you."

Jenna nodded slightly but didn't speak. Her gaze flicked toward Dr. Ford, who gave her a reassuring nod.

"Maya, thank you for being here," Dr. Ford said. "This is a safe space for both of you. There's no expectation, no pressure—just an opportunity to share and support each other."

Maya glanced at Jenna, her expression softening. "I know it feels like they took everything from you," she said. "Like you'll never feel whole again. But trust me—it gets better. It's not easy, but it's possible."

Jenna's lips pressed into a thin line, her hands twisting the hem of her sweater. "How?" she asked, her voice barely above a whisper. "How does it get better?"

Maya leaned forward slightly, her tone earnest, though her hesitation was still evident in the slight tremor in her voice. "Because you survived. They wanted to break you, but they didn't. And now, you have the power to make sure they can't do it to anyone else."

Jenna's eyes shimmered with unshed tears, her walls beginning to crack. "I don't feel powerful," she admitted. "I feel…broken."

Maya reached out, her hand resting lightly on Jenna's. "That's how they want you to feel. But you're here. You're talking. And that's more than they ever thought you'd do."

Jenna's fingers stilled under Maya's touch, the connection between them sparking a tentative sense of trust.

Jenna hesitated before asking, "How…how did you escape?"

Maya's expression darkened, but she didn't hesitate. "About 8 months ago...I jumped out of a hotel window," she said, her voice steady but filled with the weight of memory. "It was on the third floor. I broke my leg when I hit the ground, but there were people nearby. They helped me to a hospital before anyone could drag me back."

Jenna's eyes widened. "You…you jumped?"

"I had to," Maya said firmly. "I wasn't going to let them control me any longer. It hurt like hell, but that pain was worth it to get out. And you know what? The people who helped me—they didn't ask questions. They just got me out of there."

Jenna swallowed hard, her gaze dropping to her lap. "I don't think I could have done that."

"You don't know what you're capable of until you're in that moment," Maya said gently. "But you don't have to do it alone now. You've got people who care, Jenna. People who want to help you."

As the conversation progressed, Maya began to share her story. Her tone was steady, though anger simmered beneath her words.

"They moved us constantly," Maya said. "Different houses, different cities. Every time we thought we had a chance to escape, they'd remind us that we didn't. They'd hurt the others, make us watch. It wasn't just about control—it was about making us believe we didn't have a choice."

Jenna listened intently, her expression a mix of fear and understanding. "They…they made you watch too?" she asked hesitantly.

Maya nodded. "Yeah. And every time, they'd say the same thing: 'This is what happens when you don't follow the rules.'"

Jenna's gaze dropped to her lap, her voice trembling as she spoke. "I remember that…the rules. They said if we didn't obey, they'd come after our families."

Maya's jaw tightened. "That's how they kept us in line. Fear. It's their weapon of choice."

Marcus, who had been quietly observing, leaned forward slightly. "Did either of you ever see the same man more than once? Someone who seemed to be in charge?"

Maya hesitated, her gaze narrowing as she thought. "There was one guy…Vince. He was smooth, charming—acted like he owned the place."

Jenna flinched at the name, her eyes widening. "Vince Russo," she murmured. "I remember him. He… he took me to a club once."

Maya's eyes snapped to Jenna. "You too?"

Marcus's attention sharpened. "What club?"

Jenna hesitated, her breathing quickening as memories surfaced. Dr. Ford placed a comforting hand on her shoulder, helping to ground her. "It's okay, Jenna. You're safe here."

Jenna took a shaky breath. "It was…upscale. Fancy. I don't know the name, but Vince always had one of us with him. Only premium girls were taken to the club. I was one of them."

Maya's expression darkened. "I remember that. I was one of them, too. He'd parade us around like trophies, keep us at his side while he met with… clients."

Marcus's pen rushed across his notepad, each word cementing a clearer picture of Vince's role. "Did either of you see any transactions take place? Any handoffs?"

Maya nodded grimly. "Yeah. Vince set up a meeting once. The guy was rich, dressed to the nines, and he picked me for his 'first experience.' Vince made the whole thing sound like a business deal."

Jenna's face paled, her hands trembling again. "I remember that too…"

Maya reached out again, her voice firm but kind. "It wasn't your fault, Jenna. None of this was. But now, we can fight back."

Marcus let the conversation wind down naturally, careful not to push for more than the survivors were ready to share. When it was time to wrap up, he stood and addressed both women.

"Thank you," he said sincerely. "What you've shared today—it's brave, and it's invaluable. We're going to use this to bring them down."

Jenna nodded, though her expression remained uncertain. Maya, however, met his gaze with a determined glint. "Just make sure you follow through."

"I will," Marcus promised.

After the session, Marcus spoke privately with Dr. Ford in the kitchen. "They've given us a lot," he said. "Vince, the club, the way he operated—it's a lead we can act on."

Dr. Ford nodded. "But remember, Detective, they're still in the early stages of recovery. Protecting their trust is just as important as using their information."

"I understand," Marcus said.

As he left the safe house, Marcus's mind raced with the details Jenna and Maya had shared. Vince was the key to unlocking the next layer of the operation, and the club was his gateway into the world of trafficking. For the first time, Marcus felt a flicker of hope—they were closing in. But the path ahead would demand every ounce of strategy and resolve he had. The fight was far from over, but today was a step forward.

Chapter 7

The glow of neon lights spilled across the windshield as Marcus tightened his grip on the mug shot of Vince Russo, his eyes narrowing as he examined the photograph for what felt like the hundredth time. Vince's smirking face stared back at him, his slicked-back hair and smug expression giving him the look of someone who thought he was untouchable.

"Just a couple of petty drug charges," Marcus muttered, holding up the mug shot for Dana to see. "He did time, but he used it to climb. Now he's running something a hell of a lot darker."

Dana leaned over from the driver's seat, her expression skeptical as she studied the image. "Petty drug charges? And now he's running a whole network of this crap? Guess he really climbed the corporate ladder of crime."

"Guys like Russo don't just climb," Marcus replied, his voice tight. "They step on anyone and everyone to get to the top. He probably used his time inside to make connections, build his empire from the shadows."

Dana smirked grimly. "It's always the charming ones, isn't it? The ones who know how to smile while stabbing you in the back."

Marcus nodded, setting the mugshot down on the dashboard. "It's a mask. People like him only care about control. Power. It's not enough for them to succeed—they have to dominate."

Dana's gaze shifted to the club entrance in the distance. "Well, tonight we're tearing that mask off. Time to show Russo he's not as untouchable as he thinks."

Marcus allowed himself a faint smirk at her determination. "Couldn't have said it better myself."

He tightened his grip on the binoculars, fingers brushing against the cold metal as he scanned the bustling entrance of Club Arcadia. It was nearing midnight, and the exclusive club's energy was at its peak. Luxury cars pulled up one after another, their doors opening to reveal immaculately dressed patrons who sauntered toward the velvet ropes. A pair of burly bouncers flanked the entrance, their sharp eyes darting between invitations and IDs.

Marcus shifted in the seat of the unmarked sedan, his unease growing. The club wasn't just a hotspot for the city's wealthy and influential—it was also a potential hub for the trafficking network he was trying to dismantle. Jenna and Maya's testimonies had led him here, their harrowing descriptions painting Vince Russo as a key figure in this dark underworld. Russo's network, known for its ruthlessness and cunning, had its tentacles spread across the city, making it a formidable foe. Club Arcadia, they said, was one of his favorite haunts.

"Still nothing," Dana muttered beside him, her sharp eyes fixed on the entrance. She sipped her coffee, its bitter aroma filling the car. "If Russo's as flashy as the girls say, he should've shown up by now."

"He'll come. This is his stage—he's not the type to resist the spotlight."

"You sound like you've got him figured out," Dana said, arching a brow.

"Not yet," Marcus admitted. "But I've dealt with men like him before. They thrive on power and control. He'll want to make an entrance, show everyone he's untouchable."

They fell into a tense silence, the car's engine idling softly as they waited. The tension was thick as Marcus's mind cycled through the details from Jenna and Maya's accounts. Both women had described Vince Russo with striking similarity—charming, calculated, and always accompanied by a girl. The club wasn't just a place for him to flaunt his power; it was where he conducted business, scouting potential clients and victims alike.

Dana tapped the steering wheel lightly. "You ever wonder why these guys get away with it for so long?"

"All the time," Marcus replied. "It's a mix of things —money, connections, fear. People like Russo don't operate alone. They've got layers of protection, a whole system designed to keep them safe while everyone else pays the price."

A sleek black car pulled up to the curb. Marcus straightened, raising the binoculars. The driver stepped out first, a tall man in a tailored suit. He opened the passenger door, and Marcus's pulse quickened as Vince Russo emerged.

"Got him," Marcus said.

Dana grabbed her binoculars. Vince was dressed to impress, his charcoal-gray suit perfectly tailored, his dark hair slicked back. He moved with the confidence of someone who owned the world—or at least wanted everyone to think he did.

As predicted, he wasn't alone. A young woman stepped out of the car, her short black dress clinging to her slender frame. She hesitated before taking Vince's arm, her movements stiff and uncertain. Even from this distance, Marcus could see the tension in her body, the way her gaze darted nervously around the street.

"She's terrified," Dana muttered. "Look at her posture—stiff, eyes scanning for exits. She's not here by choice."

Marcus's jaw tightened. "Exactly."

The pair approached the entrance, bypassing the line entirely. The bouncers didn't even glance at their IDs, unhooking the velvet rope and waving them through. Vince exchanged a few words with one of them, his grin easy and confident. The woman beside him stayed silent, her head slightly bowed.

"They know him," Dana observed. "He's a regular."

"Of course they know him," Marcus said. "This isn't his first show."

Inside the car, the tension thickened. Marcus reached for the door handle.

"I'm going to get a closer look. Stay here and keep an eye on the entrance."

"Be careful," Dana said. "We can't afford to spook him."

Marcus slipped out of the car and into the shadows. The cool night air wrapped around him as he crossed the street, blending into the flow of pedestrians. Music pulsed from within the club, but the heavy doors and dark-tinted walls gave no hint of what was happening inside. He made a slow circle around the building, pretending to check his phone, occasionally glancing at the entrance and the side alley.

"Anything?" Dana's voice crackled in his earpiece.

Marcus kept walking, speaking low. "Place is locked up tight. No windows. No view inside. It's designed to keep people out—or keep secrets in. I'm not getting in tonight without blowing my cover."

"You should probably get back here," Dana said. "You don't want to spook anyone."

"Copy that," Marucs replied.

Back in the car, Dana handed him the binoculars. "Well? What's our next move?"

Marcus brought the binoculars to his eyes. "We wait and see what happens," he said. "They'll have to leave at some point."

As the night wore on, Marcus sifted through the mental snapshots he'd collected—faces, gestures, moments that said more than words ever could. The girl's posture alone told the truth. This wasn't luxury. It wasn't nightlife. It was captivity dressed in sequins.

"That girl," Dana said quietly, her voice threaded with fatigue, "she's scared out of her mind."

"She didn't want to be there," Marcus replied.

"We could've stopped them," she murmured.

Marcus didn't look at her. His voice stayed calm, measured. "And what then? We stop them, we lose Russo. And maybe the whole operation."

Dana fell silent. A pair of women in glittering dresses stumbled out of the club, laughing without care, high heels clicking on the pavement. To everyone else, Club Arcadia was a playground. But for girls like Isabel, it was a much darker place.

Then—movement. Near the side entrance, a man stepped out into the alley's dim light, his suit crisp, a briefcase in hand.

"This place isn't just a party scene," Marcus muttered. "It's a meeting point."

"You think he's a client?" Dana asked.

Before Marcus could answer, the side door opened again. Vince Russo stepped out with the same young woman beside him, her arm tucked through his like she had no choice. Her movements were small and hesitant, her eyes fixed on the ground.

Vince spoke quietly to the man in the suit, then opened the back door of a waiting car and gestured for the girl to get in.

She hesitated—a flicker of resistance—then climbed in without a word. The suited man followed, slipping in beside her. The car pulled away a moment later, smooth and silent. Marcus caught a clear look at the back bumper. No plate.

He shook his head. "She just got rented out to a client," he said quietly. "And all we can do right now is sit here and watch."

Dana exhaled slowly, the weight of the night pressing down. "This case is going to break a lot of people. It's already breaking me."

Marcus looked at her. "Then we don't let it. Not now. Not when we're this close."

She nodded, but her grip on the steering wheel told a different story—tight, white-knuckled.

"You ever feel like this whole thing's too big for us?" she asked quietly. "Like we're always one step behind?"

"All the time," Marcus said. "But if we let that stop us, they win. And I'm not about to let that happen."

Chapter 8

Elaine's apartment was a cluster of papers, open laptops, and pinboards adorned with maps and connections that rivaled his precinct's investigation board. Her makeshift war room was an organized chaos of financial spreadsheets, photographs, and sticky notes connecting names to events, companies, and places.

Her ability to gather information still surprised him. She was relentless, sifting through every digital footprint, corporate connection, and public record. Her small apartment felt more like an investigative bunker, every inch of it reflecting her single-minded determination to expose the truth.

"You've been busy," Marcus said, leaning back in the chair as he flipped through a printout of offshore transactions tied to the city councilman, Richard Gaines. His tone was calm, but his furrowed brow betrayed a mixture of amazement and concern.

Elaine didn't look up from her screen. "I don't take on stories halfway, Detective. When I got that lead on Elite Opportunities, I knew it was big, but I had no idea how deeply it was intertwined with the city's political and social elite."

She tapped a few keys and turned her laptop toward Marcus. A list of transactions appeared, along with scanned images of receipts, email screenshots, and a grainy photograph of Councilman Gaines shaking hands with a sharply dressed man at what seemed to be a gala.

"This is where the trail leads," Elaine said, pointing to the photo. "Gaines isn't just a politician; he's a gatekeeper. His galas and events aren't just about fundraising—they're about networking for those with… very particular interests."

Marcus studied the photograph. Gaines wore the polished grin of a career politician, but his companion caught his attention. "Who's this?" Marcus asked, tapping the screen.

Elaine smiled grimly. "That's one of his close associates. His name's Darren Calloway. He's not a trafficker himself, but he plays a significant role. He acts as a bridge between the political and the criminal. Calloway's name pops up in connection with several suspicious accounts—donations that lead back to shell companies tied to Elite Opportunities."

Marcus set the photo down and rubbed his temples. "It's a web. And Gaines is the anchor."

"Exactly," Elaine agreed. "Gaines provides the legitimacy. His events give people like Calloway and others a safe space to vet potential clients and associates."

Marcus shook his head. "How do you even find this stuff? Some of these connections are subtle—hell, some of them are buried under layers of plausible deniability."

Elaine smirked, leaning back in her chair. "Journalists don't just write stories, Detective. We dig. I have sources within city government, campaign insiders who owe me favors, and a knack for piecing things together. It's not always glamorous, but it gets results."

Marcus nodded, impressed but wary. "And you're sure about this gala? That it's one of their key meeting points?"

Elaine stood and walked to the far side of the room, retrieving a folder marked "Gala Intel." She handed it to Marcus, her expression serious. "It's not just any gala. There's one happening in two weeks, and it's one of the biggest charity events of the year. Publicly, it's about supporting at-risk youth programs and housing initiatives. Privately? It's where the city's wealthiest gather to discuss things they don't want on record."

Flipping through the folder, Marcus saw promotional flyers for the gala, a list of confirmed attendees, and a detailed breakdown of security measures. "It's open to anyone who can pay for a ticket," Elaine continued, "but there's a hidden layer—a special booth for 'select' guests. That's where the real networking happens."

Marcus leaned back, his mind racing. "So this booth…it's like a VIP section for traffickers and their clients?"

"Essentially," Elaine confirmed. "It's where they vet new faces, build trust, and expand their network. And if I'm right, that's where you need to be."

Marcus raised an eyebrow. "And how do you suggest I get there? I can't just walk in and announce my intentions."

Elaine grinned, walking over to her desk and pulling out another folder. "That's where I come in."

She laid the folder in front of him, and Marcus opened it to find a meticulously crafted alias. Business cards, financial records, a backstory—it was all there.

"Meet Logan Harper," Elaine said, leaning over the desk. "Mid-level entrepreneur with a penchant for exclusive events and a history of shady but profitable ventures. Harper has just enough clout to pique their interest but not enough notoriety to raise alarms."

Marcus stared at the documents, impressed despite himself. "You've been busy."

Elaine shrugged. "I had time, and I figured you'd need something airtight. Harper's background checks out in all the right places. I've planted digital breadcrumbs—enough to back up the story if they dig."

"And you're confident this will work?" Marcus asked.

Elaine met his gaze, her expression unwavering. "If you play the part right, yes. You'll need to network, drop subtle hints about your 'interests,' and make them come to you. These people thrive on discretion and exclusivity. You show them you can keep up, and they'll open the door."

Marcus exhaled sharply, the weight of the plan settling on him. "It's risky. If I slip up, I'll blow my cover—and the case."

Elaine's expression softened. "I know. But it's the best shot we have. You've been chasing these people from the outside for months. This is your chance to get inside."

Marcus nodded slowly, flipping through the alias materials again. "And the gala?"

"I'll secure your ticket and make sure your name's on the right list," Elaine said. "It's public enough to avoid suspicion but exclusive enough to require connections. You'll blend right in."

She paused, her expression turning serious. "But understand this—if you get in and something goes wrong, there won't be a second chance. You won't get invited again. They'll disappear before we can find them."

Marcus nodded, the weight of her words settling deep. "Then I won't screw it up."

The room fell silent as Marcus absorbed the enormity of the plan. Finally, he looked up at Elaine. "You're putting yourself in a lot of danger for this."

Elaine smirked. "You're not the only one who wants to see these bastards taken down, Detective. Besides,

I've been doing this for a long time. I know how to stay under the radar."

Marcus set the folder down, his resolve hardening. "Then let's do it. But we do this my way—no shortcuts, no unnecessary risks."

Elaine hesitated for just a moment, then she nodded. "Agreed. And Marcus? Be careful. These people don't just play dirty—they play for keeps."

As Marcus left Elaine's apartment that night, the weight of the operation bore down on him. He had his alias, his entry point, and his first real chance to infiltrate the network. But he also knew the risks. One misstep, one moment of hesitation, and it could all fall apart.

Still, as he walked into the cool night air, a flicker of determination burned in his chest. The traffickers had built their empire on fear and secrecy. Now, it was Marcus's turn to step into their world—and tear it apart from the inside.

* * *

Marcus stepped into the precinct early the next morning, his mind still racing from the plan Elaine Monroe had laid out. As he settled at his desk, Dana appeared, holding two cups of coffee. She set one down in front of him without a word, her sharp eyes scanning his tired face.

"Late night?" Dana asked, leaning on the desk.

"Something like that," Marcus replied, taking a sip of the coffee.

Dana raised an eyebrow. "You've got that look again—the one you get when you're about to do something reckless."

Marcus smirked faintly but didn't respond. Instead, he handed her a folder containing the information Elaine had compiled. "Take a look at this."

Dana opened the folder, her expression shifting as she flipped through the documents. "Councilman Richard Gaines?" she said, frowning at the pages. "What's this about?"

"Elaine's been digging," Marcus said. "She found a trail of financial transactions and connections that tie him to Elite Opportunities. He's hosting a gala in two weeks, and it's more than just a charity event. Gaines is one of their key players—someone who helps facilitate introductions and keeps things running smoothly."

Dana's eyes narrowed. "So, he's not just a corrupt politician. He's a gatekeeper."

"Exactly," Marcus confirmed. "We need to dig into his connections—phone records, campaign donors, anything that ties him directly to Elite Opportunities."

Dana nodded slowly, her focus shifting to the folder again. "And you think this gala is important?"

"I do," Marcus said. "It's where they bring people together—clients, facilitators, enforcers. If we can figure out who else is attending, it might give us a better picture of the network."

Dana closed the folder and looked at him. "I'll start pulling what I can. But, Marcus, this feels bigger than what we're used to. Be careful."

Marcus gave her a reassuring nod. "Always."

Chapter 9

Marcus adjusted the cufflinks on his tailored suit as he stepped out of the hired car and onto the marble steps leading to the Brighton Manor. The grand, opulent venue towered before him, its glittering chandeliers visible through expansive floor-to-ceiling windows. Guests in flowing gowns and expertly tailored tuxedos milled about the entrance, exchanging polite conversation as they waited for their invitations to be validated.

He tightened his grip on the sleek, black-embossed invitation that bore the name "Logan Harper," the alias meticulously crafted by Elaine Monroe. The past weeks of preparation had all led to this moment. Tonight,

Marcus wasn't a detective; he was Harper—a mid-level entrepreneur with deep pockets and a taste for exclusivity.

As he approached the doorman, Marcus adopted the air of practiced indifference Elaine had drilled into him. He handed over the invitation, ignoring the brief scrutiny from the man before being waved through with a polite, "Welcome, Mr. Harper. Enjoy the evening."

The foyer of Brighton Manor opened into a sprawling ballroom that radiated wealth and power. The scent of expensive perfumes and colognes mingled in the air, adding to the opulence. The space was a kaleidoscope of lavish floral arrangements, rich fabrics, and designer jewelry. A string quartet played a hauntingly beautiful melody from a corner, their music barely audible over the hum of conversation.

Marcus paused just inside the entrance, taking in the room with a casual gaze that belied his sharp focus. Every detail mattered tonight. He needed to understand the dynamics of the crowd, the hierarchy of power, and the unspoken rules that governed this hidden world. More importantly, he needed to find Darren Calloway —the bridge between Councilman Richard Gaines and Vince Russo.

Moving toward the bar, Marcus passed clusters of guests engaged in animated discussion. He recognized a few faces from Elaine's briefings: prominent business leaders, socialites, and politicians, including Councilman Gaines himself. Gaines stood near the stage, surrounded by admirers, his polished demeanor masking the corruption Marcus now knew lurked beneath.

At the bar, Marcus ordered a whiskey neat, his choice deliberate. Elaine had advised him to avoid anything that might seem overly pretentious or ostentatious. "Logan Harper is understated," she'd said. "Confident but not flashy. He's the kind of man who lets his wallet do the talking."

Marcus sipped his drink as he surveyed the room. He spotted Darren Calloway near a group of guests by the silent auction display. Calloway was everything Elaine had described—charming, well-dressed, and exuding the effortless confidence of someone who knew he was untouchable. He moved between conversations with ease, his smile never faltering, his laugh always perfectly timed. Marcus noted the way Calloway's eyes darted around the room, constantly assessing, always in control.

It wasn't time to approach Calloway just yet. Marcus needed to establish a presence first, to blend in rather than stand out as a newcomer. He began mingling, introducing himself to other guests with the practiced ease of someone used to networking. Every handshake, every polite exchange added to the illusion of Logan Harper's existence.

After half an hour, Marcus positioned himself near one of the ornate display tables, which featured auction items. A delicate painting caught his attention—not because of its artistic merit but because Darren Calloway had wandered over to examine it.

"Quite the piece, isn't it?" Calloway said casually, his voice smooth.

Marcus glanced up, feigning mild surprise. "It is," he said, stepping aside slightly to give Calloway room. "I'm more of an appreciator than a collector, though."

Calloway chuckled. "A man who knows his limits. I can respect that." He extended a hand. "Darren Calloway."

"Logan Harper," Marcus replied, shaking Calloway's hand. "Pleasure to meet you."

"And you," Calloway said, his sharp eyes studying Marcus with interest. "New to these events, I take it?"

Marcus gave a slight shrug, letting a faint smile play on his lips. "First time at this particular gala, yes. However, I've visited a few others in my time. I'm always interested in making the right connections."

Calloway's smile widened slightly. "And what kind of connections would those be?"

Marcus hesitated just long enough to appear thoughtful. "The kind that isn't discussed in polite company."

The faintest glimmer of approval flickered in Calloway's expression. "You're in the right place, Mr. Harper. Though I'll warn you, discretion is highly valued here. This isn't the kind of crowd that takes kindly to loose talk or idle curiosity."

"I wouldn't have come if I didn't understand that," Marcus said evenly, meeting Calloway's gaze without flinching. "I value discretion as much as anyone in this room."

Calloway nodded, clearly intrigued. "Then perhaps we'll find an opportunity to speak later. For now, enjoy the evening."

Marcus inclined his head, letting Calloway move on without pressing the conversation further. It was a delicate dance, one that required patience and precision.

Marcus knew that if he pushed too hard or seemed too eager, he could lose everything.

Over the next hour, Marcus continued to navigate the room, his movements calculated and deliberate. He engaged in small talk, offered polite smiles, and gradually allowed Logan Harper to become a fixture of the gala. His strategic approach was evident in every move, his eyes always on Calloway, noting the people he spoke to and the subtle signals that passed between them.

Finally, as the night began to wind down, Marcus found himself once again near Calloway, this time by the bar. Calloway turned to him with a faint smile. "Still enjoying yourself, Mr. Harper?"

"Very much," Marcus replied. "Though I must admit, these events can be a bit overwhelming. So many faces, so many conversations—it's hard to know where to start."

Calloway chuckled. "You're not wrong. But if I may offer some advice—it's not about how many people you speak to. It's about who you speak to."

Marcus raised an eyebrow, playing along. "And how does one go about finding the right people?"

Calloway studied him for a moment, his expression unreadable. Then, with a satisfied nod, he gestured toward a quieter corner of the room. "Walk with me."

Marcus followed, his pulse steady but his senses on high alert. The two men wove through the crowd, eventually stopping near a grand fireplace adorned with marble sculptures. The noise of the room softened here, offering a semblance of privacy.

"You're an interesting man, Mr. Harper," Calloway began, his tone casual but probing. "Not many people walk into these events with your confidence. You carry yourself like someone who knows how to get what he wants."

"I've found that confidence opens doors," Marcus replied evenly. "But I also know that some doors aren't meant to be approached head-on."

Calloway raised an eyebrow, clearly intrigued. "And what doors are you hoping to open tonight?"

Marcus allowed a small smile to play on his lips. "The kind that requires introductions. I'm a firm believer in the value of connections, Mr. Calloway. And from what I've seen, you're a man who knows how to make them."

Calloway chuckled, clearly pleased. "You've done your homework, Mr. Harper."

"I wouldn't be here otherwise," Marcus said simply.

Calloway swirled his champagne, his gaze thoughtful. "You strike me as a man who values discretion. Am I right?"

"Absolutely," Marcus replied. "Without discretion, there's no trust. And without trust, there's no business."

Calloway nodded slowly, his smile returning. "Good. Because discretion is everything in my world. You might say it's the currency we trade in."

Marcus inclined his head, maintaining the air of calm confidence that Elaine had drilled into him. Every word and every gesture had to be calculated. This was the moment when the entire operation could rise or fall.

"I like you, Mr. Harper," Calloway said finally. "You've got the right instincts. But trust isn't something I give lightly. It's earned."

Marcus leaned slightly closer, his tone low but steady. "Tell me how, and I'll prove myself."

For a fraction of a second, Marcus wondered if he'd overplayed his hand. Had he shown too much eagerness? Too little? In this room, mistakes were made in whispers. Calloway studied him in silence, and Marcus kept his posture relaxed, his breathing steady, masking the ripple of tension beneath his skin.

Calloway's smile grew sharper. He reached into his jacket pocket and produced a sleek black card embossed with gold lettering. "For individuals who value discretion and exclusivity," he began, "there's a place I believe you'll find...interesting. Visit this club, ask for Vincent, and use this card. Tell him Darren sent you."

Marcus accepted the card, his pulse steady despite the weight of the moment. "I appreciate the introduction."

Calloway's eyes held his for a beat longer than necessary. "Just make sure you don't waste it, Mr. Harper. Opportunities like this don't come twice."

The warning was barely veiled, wrapped in charm, and delivered with a smile—but it landed all the same.

"I won't," Marcus said evenly.

"Good," Calloway replied, already turning away. "We'll see where it leads."

With that, Calloway stepped away, leaving Marcus with the invitation in hand. He slipped the card into his pocket as he exited the gala, the cool night air offering a brief moment of calm. His mind raced as he considered the implications of the night's success—and the dangers still to come.

Less than an hour later, Marcus sat in Elaine's cluttered apartment. She leaned against the table, arms crossed, watching Marcus as he produced the invitation from his pocket and set it down in front of her.

"It worked," he said simply, his voice carrying satisfaction.

Elaine picked up the card, studying it intently. "Darren Calloway. It's exactly what we needed," she said, though her tone held a note of caution. "This gets you into Vince Russo's club, but Marcus, this isn't just a door—it's a trap if you're not careful."

Marcus rubbed the back of his neck, his mind still racing from the night's events. "I know. But it's our only way forward."

Elaine hesitated, setting the card back down. "The stakes keep getting higher, Detective. You're walking into their world now. If they even sense you're not who you say you are..."

"I know," Marcus interrupted. "That's why I need to make sure this alias holds up. Everything hinges on Logan Harper being airtight."

Elaine studied him for a moment, then nodded. "I'll double-check everything tonight. But, Marcus, once you're in, it's up to you to maintain your cover. You're the only one who can pull this off."

Marcus stood, slipping the card back into his pocket. "Thanks, Elaine. For everything. I'll keep you in the loop."

Elaine followed him to the door, her concern evident in her eyes. "Just remember," she said quietly, "you're not invincible, Marcus. You can't help anyone if you don't make it out of this alive."

Marcus gave a faint smirk, though his eyes reflected the weight of her words. "I'll be careful."

As he stepped out into the night, the city's lights reflecting off the damp pavement, Marcus knew the path ahead would test him in ways he couldn't yet predict. The invitation was just the beginning.

Chapter 10

Marcus stood in his office, his gaze fixed on the whiteboard covered in a sprawling network of evidence. The door creaked open, and Dana stepped inside, a file in one hand and a guarded expression on her face.

"You've been staring at that thing all morning?" she asked, nodding toward the whiteboard.

Marcus gave a faint shrug, not looking away. "Trying to make the pieces fit. Still a few too many blanks."

Dana set the folder down on his desk. "You've got that look. The one you get when something's chewing at you."

He turned slowly, meeting her gaze. For a moment, he didn't speak.

"You remember when I asked you to keep that meeting with Dr. Ford off the record?" he said finally.

Dana arched a brow. "Hard to forget. You were borderline paranoid."

"I had to be," Marcus replied. He stepped away from the board and leaned back against his desk, arms crossed. "This next part goes even deeper. And it's a hell of a lot more dangerous."

Dana's eyes narrowed. "Okay. I'm listening."

Marcus hesitated, choosing his words with care. "Elaine Monroe and I...we've been working on something. An undercover angle. We created an alias— Logan Harper. Businessman. Looks clean on the outside but dirty enough under the surface to fit in with Russo's people."

Dana blinked. "You created a fake identity? With Elaine?"

"It's airtight," Marcus said. "Financials, background, everything. She built it from the ground up. And last night, I used it to get into the Brighton Manor gala."

Dana's mouth parted slightly. "You're telling me you went to that thing alone—and you're just now saying something?"

"I needed to make sure it worked before pulling anyone else in," he said.

She glared at him. "You're lucky you didn't get yourself killed. And Monroe? She's calling the shots now?"

"She's not running the show," Marcus corrected. "She's giving me the tools I need. That alias got me in front of Darren Calloway. He gave me a card. An invitation to Russo's club. That's where I'm headed next."

Dana leaned back, arms crossed tight. "So now you're going straight into the lion's den. Alone."

"That's why I need you," Marcus said. "Outside. Watching my back. If something goes wrong, I need someone I trust to get me out."

"Does the chief know about any of this?"

Marcus shook his head. "No. And it's going to stay that way."

Dana let out a low breath. "Marcus, that's a big gamble. You're walking a razor's edge."

"I know," he said simply. "But it's the only way forward."

Dana exhaled and leaned against the edge of his desk. "You really don't think Nash should be in on this?

He's not the enemy, Marcus. If something goes sideways, he's the one who could pull strings."

Marcus shook his head. "Going by the book is what they expect. If word of Harper leaks, the whole thing crumbles. Nash would do the right thing—and that's exactly the problem."

Dana frowned, arms crossed tightly. "You're asking me to back you on something that could blow up in both our faces."

"I'm asking you to help me stop them before we have to deal with more dead girls," Marcus said. "If we don't do this now, we might not get another chance."

She studied him for a long moment, then finally sighed. "All right," she said, "but if you screw up, and I'm hauling your ass out of there, alias be damned."

"Fair enough," Marcus said. He glanced at the clock on his desk, the weight of the upcoming operation pressing heavily on him. "Let's reconvene tomorrow and finalize the logistics."

Dana stood, her expression still tense. "You're playing a dangerous game, Marcus. Don't let Monroe push you too far."

"She's not pushing me," Marcus said firmly. "This is my choice."

Dana didn't look convinced, but she nodded anyway. "Just don't get yourself killed. We can't afford to lose you."

Marcus returned to his notes after Dana left, his focus narrowing to the club. There were still too many unknowns, but one thing was clear—tomorrow, he'd be stepping into enemy territory. And if he wasn't careful, it could be his last move.

* * *

The city lights reflected off Marcus's polished shoes as he stepped out of the unmarked car parked discreetly in an alley a block from Vince Russo's exclusive club. The muted hum of nightlife echoed around him, blending with the distant wail of a siren. Despite the city's buzz, the street outside the club felt insulated, as if the world inside operated on its own set of rules.

Dana leaned against the hood of her sedan, arms crossed and a scowl etched on her face. She watched Marcus approach, her eyes narrowing as he adjusted his tie and straightened his jacket. "You really look the part," she said, her tone begrudging. "I don't know if I want to applaud Elaine for crafting this Logan Harper persona or drag her into this alley and tell her to stop encouraging you."

Marcus smirked faintly. "I'll let her know you're impressed."

"Don't push it," Dana muttered, running a hand through her short hair. "I still think this whole thing is insane. You're walking into a room full of people who wouldn't think twice about killing you if they even suspect you're a cop."

"That's why we've spent weeks preparing," Marcus replied. "No one inside that club will have a reason to question me."

Dana frowned, her skepticism evident. "You're betting a lot on that."

"It's a calculated risk," Marcus said firmly. "And it's one I have to take. If we don't get closer to Vince, this case will keep going in circles."

Dana threw her hands up in frustration. "And you think you're the one who has to do it? Have you thought about what happens if you slip up? If someone asks the wrong question or sees something that doesn't add up?"

"I have," Marcus admitted. "That's why I need you out here. If something goes wrong, you call it in. SWAT, backup—whatever it takes."

Dana shook her head, pacing a few steps away. Marcus followed her movements, his tone softening. "You think I want to do this, Dana? You think I enjoy walking into a place like that and pretending to be one of them? I don't. But if this is what it takes to bring these bastards down, then I'll do it."

For a moment, neither of them spoke. The weight of the situation hung heavily between them, unspoken fears lingering just beneath the surface.

Finally, Dana sighed and gestured to the car. "All right. Let's run through this one more time. Humor me."

Marcus nodded, his patience intact. "Fine. Let's go over it."

They moved to the hood of her car, where Dana had spread out a crude map of the surrounding area. She tapped the club's location, marked with a red circle.

"You go in," Dana began, her finger tracing a path to the entrance. "You flash that fancy card Calloway gave you, and they let you through. Once you're inside, stick to the plan—don't ask questions, don't offer more than necessary, and avoid getting too friendly. These people thrive on suspicion. The less you say, the better."

"Understood," Marcus said. "And if someone gets too curious?"

"Deflect," Dana said. "Use your backstory. Harper's a businessman, right? Make them think you're here to spend money and nothing else."

Marcus smirked. "I'm starting to think you're better at this than I am."

"I'd rather be in there than out here," Dana muttered. "But someone's got to pull your ass out of the fire if it comes to that."

She pointed to a nearby alleyway. "I'll be parked here, engine running. If you need out, three taps on the watch."

Marcus gave a slight nod. "Signal goes straight to your phone. I remember."

"Good," Dana said. "But you better be damn sure. If we go in guns blazing and it turns out to be nothing—"

"I know the stakes," Marcus said, cutting her off gently. "I won't signal unless it's life or death."

Dana nodded, though her tension didn't ease. She folded her arms and leaned against the car, studying him for a long moment.

"You really believe this is going to work?" she asked quietly.

"I have to," Marcus replied. "It's the only shot we've got."

Dana exhaled sharply. "You're too damn stubborn for your own good, you know that?"

"So I've been told," Marcus said with a faint smile.

He stepped back and turned toward the club. His heart pounded in his chest, but his steps were steady, his mind focused. He wasn't Detective Marcus Cole tonight. He was Logan Harper, a man chasing shadows in a world where trust was currency and mistakes were fatal.

As he approached the glowing awning of the club, the sound of his footsteps on the pavement seemed to echo louder than before. He tightened his grip on the sleek black card in his pocket, the weight of the operation pressing heavily on his shoulders.

Behind him, Dana watched from the car, her hand resting on the steering wheel as she whispered to herself, "Don't screw this up, Marcus."

The club's bouncer stepped aside as Marcus reached the entrance and presented his invitation, his sharp gaze briefly scanning him before nodding. Marcus didn't hesitate. He took a deep breath, straightened his tie, and stepped forward, leaving the cool night air behind.

Chapter 11

The soft hum of jazz music greeted Marcus as he stepped into the dimly lit club, his polished shoes sinking slightly into the thick, opulent carpet. Every detail of the club's interior screamed exclusivity —from the crystal chandeliers casting muted golden light to the intricately carved wooden paneling lining the walls. Marcus, fully immersed in his alias as Logan Harper, exuded a calm detachment as he surveyed the space. His posture was relaxed, his tailored suit perfectly fitted, and his expression unreadable. Calloway's recommendation had gotten him this far, but he knew that everything from this moment forward depended on his ability to convince Vince Russo he belonged.

A hostess dressed in a sleek black gown approached, her smile professional but her eyes sharp, assessing him in an instant. "Mr. Harper," she said smoothly. "Welcome to the club. Mr. Russo is expecting you. May I take your coat?"

Marcus nodded, slipping off his dark overcoat and handing it to her without hesitation. "Thank you."

"Right this way," she said, gesturing for him to follow.

The club's main floor was a sprawling labyrinth of luxury. Groups of well-dressed patrons reclined on plush leather sofas or leaned against polished marble bars. Glasses of fine whiskey, champagne, and wine glittered in their hands as quiet conversations hummed through the space. The room was filled with a deceptive sense of ease. Still, Marcus didn't miss the subtle nods, guarded whispers, or occasional glances exchanged among certain guests. Beneath the surface of civility, this was a hunting ground for the powerful and corrupt.

The hostess led him down a hallway lined with curtained booths, each one offering more privacy than the last. Soft laughter and muffled voices drifted through the heavy fabric, hinting at the clandestine discussions taking place within. Marcus's instincts were on high alert, but he maintained the practiced poise of a man accustomed to such surroundings.

At the end of the hallway stood a solid oak door flanked by two imposing men in dark suits. Both had the unmistakable build of professional enforcers, their expressions blank but their eyes constantly scanning. One of them stepped forward as the hostess stopped, giving a slight nod.

"This is Mr. Harper," she said. "He's expected."

The guard stepped aside and opened the door without a word. Marcus followed the hostess inside, entering a private lounge that was both understated and opulent. The room was dominated by a large leather sectional couch, a glass coffee table, and a fully stocked bar to one side. Subtle ambient lighting cast long shadows across the walls, creating a warm and intimate atmosphere.

Vince Russo stood near the bar, pouring himself a glass of what appeared to be bourbon. He was impeccably dressed, his tailored suit emphasizing his sharp frame and exuding effortless sophistication. His dark hair was slicked back, and his smile was as polished as the glass in his hand. Vince turned as

Marcus entered, his piercing gaze locking onto him like a hawk assessing prey.

Sitting on the couch beside Vince was a young woman, likely no older than twenty. She wore an elegant black dress that clung to her frame, her makeup flawless, and her expression carefully blank. Marcus didn't miss the subtle tension in her posture, the way her hands rested stiffly in her lap. She was a premium girl, paraded as part of Vince's image of power and control.

"Mr. Harper," Vince said, his voice smooth and welcoming. "It's a pleasure to finally meet you."

Marcus inclined his head, allowing a faint smile to touch his lips. "The pleasure's mine, Vince. I've heard a lot about you."

"All good things, I hope," Vince replied with a chuckle, motioning toward the couch. "Please, sit. Make yourself comfortable."

Marcus moved to the couch, lowering himself into one corner with a relaxed air. Vince joined him, sitting across the glass coffee table and setting his drink down. For a moment, there was silence as Vince studied Marcus, his sharp eyes missing nothing. Marcus met his gaze evenly, understanding the unspoken test unfolding between them.

"I have to admit," Vince said, leaning back slightly, "Darren's recommendation caught my attention. He doesn't vouch for just anyone. What exactly did you say to impress him?"

Marcus allowed a faint smirk to play on his lips. "I didn't say anything. Darren's the kind of man who appreciates actions more than words."

Vince's eyebrows lifted slightly, his smile widening. "Good answer. But now I'm curious—what actions are you hoping to take here?"

Marcus leaned forward slightly, resting his forearms on his knees. "That depends. I've heard this is the kind of place where connections are made. The kind that isn't found anywhere else."

"You've heard right," Vince said, his tone turning serious. "But connections require trust, Logan. And trust isn't given lightly in this world."

"I wouldn't expect otherwise," Marcus replied smoothly. "And I'm not here to waste your time, Vince. I wouldn't have come this far if I were not serious."

Vince studied him for a moment longer before nodding slowly. "All right. Let's see if you're as serious as you claim."

He leaned forward and picked up a sleek tablet from the coffee table, unlocking it with a quick tap. The screen illuminated, revealing a digital payment form. Vince turned it toward Marcus, his expression unreadable. "A deposit," he said simply. "Twenty-five thousand. Consider it a down payment for the opportunities ahead."

Marcus's pulse quickened, but he kept his expression neutral. This was the moment he'd been prepared for, the test that would determine whether he could step deeper into Vince's world.

"Reasonable," Marcus said, entering the account details displayed on the tablet. Every keystroke felt like a nail in the coffin, but he forced himself to remain calm. The transfer confirmation appeared on his phone, and he held it up briefly before setting it down on the table.

"It's done," he said.

Vince glanced at the tablet, a pleased smile crossing his face as the payment registered. "Efficient. I like that."

Marcus inclined his head slightly, his demeanor steady despite the churn of his thoughts. "I've found that efficiency is an underrated virtue."

Vince laughed softly, picking up his drink and taking a slow sip. "I think you and I are going to get along just fine, Logan. But tell me—what exactly are you looking for here? What piqued your interest in my operation?"

Marcus allowed a brief pause, crafting his answer carefully. "Discretion," he said finally. "And exclusivity. I'm tired of dealing with amateurs, Vince. I need people who understand the value of both."

Vince's smile turned sharper, though his eyes were like cold steel, cutting into Marcus's every move. "You've come to the right place," Vince said smoothly, his tone laced with both invitation and menace. "But let's cut the pleasantries, Logan. What's your taste? Specifics matter in my business."

Marcus forced himself to appear unbothered, leaning back in his seat. The room felt stifling, the air charged with tension. This was the moment he'd dreaded since walking into the club. The casual way Vince spoke about human lives—reducing them to commodities—twisted Marcus's stomach, but he had no choice but to respond in kind.

He dropped his gaze for a moment as if contemplating, then met Vince's eyes with calculated resolve. "I'm not looking for the dime-a-dozen types," Marcus said, lowering his voice as if sharing a dirty secret. "I want something fresh. Young. Innocent but trainable."

The words tasted like bile, but Marcus didn't flinch. He knew Vince would be watching for any hint of hesitation or discomfort. Every second stretched painfully, but Marcus leaned into the role, channeling the indifference Elaine had drilled into him.

Vince tilted his head, his expression sharpening as he studied Marcus. "Young, huh? How young are we talking?"

Marcus's jaw tightened, though he masked it with a faint, forced smirk. "Nothing that draws the wrong kind of attention. Sixteen, seventeen—old enough to follow orders but young enough to keep the appeal."

Vince's eyes narrowed slightly, then he chuckled darkly, swirling his glass of bourbon. "You know, some guys come in here pretending they're better than that. They skirt around what they really want, hoping I'll do the dirty work for them. I don't deal in half-truths, Logan. You? You get right to the point. I respect that."

Marcus gave a short nod, keeping his expression neutral. Inside, he could feel his pulse pounding, his body taut with tension. Vince's approval was necessary, but it felt like walking a razor's edge, one wrong word away from exposing his cover.

"Here's the thing about this business," Vince continued, setting his drink down and leaning forward.

"It's not just about taste—it's about trust. If I'm going to bring you into my world, I need to know you're serious. And that you're not gonna get squeamish when things get...complicated."

Marcus mirrored Vince's movement, leaning in slightly and meeting his gaze. "I don't get squeamish, Vince. I get results."

Vince's laugh was low and cold, echoing softly in the room. "You're starting to grow on me, Logan. But talk is cheap. Actions prove loyalty. You've taken the first step with that deposit, but if you want to play in my league, there's more to it than money."

Marcus arched an eyebrow, feigning intrigue. "What are you suggesting?"

Vince's smile turned predatory. "Let's just say there's a test coming. One that'll show me exactly how far you're willing to go to be part of this.

Marcus frowned, "A test?

"Don't worry yourself over it," Vince replied. "But in the meantime, I'll arrange something special for you. A meeting at the Regency Hotel—suite 514. Be there tomorrow night at nine sharp. A little treat will be waiting for you. I think you'll like her."

Marcus nodded, forcing a confident smile. "I'll be there."

Vince leaned back again, satisfied. "Good. Stick to your lane, have a good time, and we'll get along just fine."

The conversation ended with an unsettling air of finality, Vince's words hanging in the room like a warning. Marcus felt the full weight of his deception pressing down on him, but he maintained his composure, knowing that every step brought him closer to exposing the network—and the man sitting across from him.

Marcus left Vince's private lounge with the heavy weight of the conversation still pressing on his shoulders. He paused near the main bar, pretending to survey the crowd while giving himself a moment to collect his thoughts. He caught sight of several familiar faces—people Elaine's research had flagged as influential figures tied to the network. They laughed, toasted, and exchanged pleasantries, blissfully unaware of the storm brewing around them.

As he made his way toward the exit, he felt the faintest tug of relief. The first phase of his mission was complete. He had secured Vince's trust—or at least enough of it to move forward. But the weight of what lay ahead was undeniable. Vince's parting words echoed in his mind: "Stick to your lane, Logan, and we'll get along just fine."

Marcus pushed open the heavy doors of the club and stepped into the crisp night air. The contrast was stark—the noise and decadence of the club giving way to the quiet hum of the city streets. He spotted the car parked discreetly a block away, the glow of the dashboard light signaling Dana's presence.

As he approached, Dana stepped out of the car, her expression a mix of relief and tension. She leaned against the driver's side door, crossing her arms as Marcus reached her.

"Well?" Dana asked, her tone sharp. "How did it go?"

Marcus exhaled, running a hand through his hair. "I'm in. Vince bought the story, and I've got a meeting tomorrow night."

Dana's brows knitted together. "A meeting? With whom?"

"I believe one of their victims," Marcus said, his voice heavy. "I don't know who or what to expect yet, but it's happening at a hotel."

Dana's jaw tightened, and she shook her head. "Jesus, Marcus. This is getting deeper than I thought. What if it's a setup? What if Vince is just testing you?"

"He is," Marcus said flatly. "Everything about tonight was a test. And so far, I've passed. But I need you to stay sharp. If something goes wrong tomorrow, I'll need backup."

Dana sighed, her frustration evident. "I still don't like this, Marcus.

Marcus nodded, his expression grim. "I know."

Dana searched his face, her eyes softening slightly. "Are you okay?"

For a moment, Marcus hesitated, the mask of Logan Harper slipping just enough to reveal the strain beneath. "I'm fine," he said quietly. "It's just…hard. Pretending to be someone like that. Listening to the way Vince talks about those girls—it's…" He trailed off, shaking his head.

Dana placed a hand on his shoulder. "I know. But you're doing this for them. For the ones who can't speak for themselves."

Marcus nodded, steeling himself. "I know. And I'm not stopping until we take them down."

Dana squeezed his shoulder before stepping back. "Just promise me you'll be careful. If they find out who you really are…"

"They won't," Marcus said firmly. "As long as we stick to the plan, they won't."

With that, Marcus opened the car door and slid into the passenger seat. Dana followed, settling behind the wheel. As the car pulled away from the curb, Marcus allowed himself a brief moment of quiet. The night's events had taken their toll, but the mission wasn't over. Tomorrow would bring new challenges, and he needed to be ready.

Chapter 12

The opulent marble floor of the luxury hotel lobby shimmered under the soft glow of crystal chandeliers. Marcus, deeply immersed in his alias as Logan Harper, strode across the space with measured confidence. His tailored suit, loosened tie, and composed demeanor were all calculated elements of the role he had to play. Yet beneath the surface, his mind churned, every step feeling heavier as he approached the night's grim objective.

A clerk behind the front desk offered him a polite nod, and Marcus returned the gesture with a faint smile. Vince Russo's arrangement ensured his arrival would raise no questions. Everything about this place exuded exclusivity—a deceptive façade that concealed the horrors lurking in its shadows. Marcus bypassed the desk, heading directly to the elevators.

Inside the mirrored elevator, Marcus adjusted his tie, the slightly askew knot, and mussed hair, completing the illusion of Logan Harper. He met his reflection, his gaze steady despite the storm brewing within him. Every detail had been calculated to sell the role, but the dissonance between the man in the mirror and who he truly was gnawed at him. His heart raced, a mix of fear and determination coursing through his veins.

The soft chime of the elevator pulled him back. The doors opened to a plush, carpeted corridor with muted lighting. Marcus stepped out and made his way to Room 514 at the far end of the hallway. The air felt thick with tension, his every step muffled by the luxurious carpet.

When he reached the door, he knocked twice. A moment later, it swung open to reveal a broad-shouldered man in a dark suit. The guard's expression was unreadable as he sized up Marcus with a single, sharp glance.

"Mr. Harper," the man said simply, stepping aside.

Marcus inclined his head and entered the room.

The suite was lavish, boasting floor-to-ceiling windows that overlooked the city skyline. Silken sheets adorned the large bed, and the subtle scent of perfume lingered in the air—a meticulously calculated effort to set the stage. None of it mattered to Marcus. His focus was on the young woman standing by the bed.

She was petite, her dark hair neatly styled, her silk robe hanging loosely around her delicate frame. Her makeup had been applied with precision, but it couldn't mask the wariness in her eyes. She stood stiffly, her hands clasped tightly in front of her, avoiding Marcus's gaze.

The guard lingered by the door, his presence a quiet reminder of the watchful eyes on them. Marcus turned his attention to him. "I assume I'll have privacy?"

The guard nodded. "Call if you need anything."

Without another word, the man stepped out, closing the door behind him. The lock clicked softly, echoing in the silence.

Marcus turned back to the girl. She still hadn't moved, her eyes fixed on a point somewhere past his shoulder.

"Mr. Harper," she said, her voice soft and steady but with a rehearsed precision. "I'm Lila. How can I please you?"

The question struck Marcus like a blow, but he forced himself to remain composed. He crossed the room and placed his phone and wallet on the desk, his movements deliberate. "Relax," he said calmly. "We're not in a rush."

Lila hesitated, then nodded mechanically. She took a small step forward, her hands moving to untie the sash of her robe.

"Wait," Marcus said, raising a hand.

She froze instantly, her wide eyes darting to his face. "Did I…do something wrong?"

"No," Marcus replied quickly, softening his tone. "Not at all. I just…I need to talk to you first."

Her brow furrowed, confusion breaking through her mask of compliance. "Talk?"

"Yes," Marcus said, motioning to the chair across from the bed. "Please. Sit."

Lila hesitated, her hands clutching the sash tightly. "This is a test, isn't it?" she whispered, her voice trembling. "To see if I follow the rules."

"No," Marcus said firmly, leaning forward slightly to meet her gaze. "This isn't a test. I'm not here to hurt you, Lila. I'm here to help."

Her eyes narrowed with suspicion. "Help? What do you mean?"

"I'm not a client," Marcus said. "I'm a detective working undercover to bring down Vince Russo and his entire operation."

Lila's breath hitched. She took a step back, glancing at the door. "This is a trick," she said, her voice rising. "They sent you to see if I'd talk—"

"It's not a trick," Marcus interrupted, his tone calm but urgent. "I know you have no reason to trust me, but I'm telling you the truth. I need your help."

Her chest rose and fell with rapid breaths. "If they find out—"

"They won't," Marcus assured her. "But I need you to tell me what you know. Anything about Vince, the places they keep you, the people involved—it could save lives."

Lila remained frozen, her wide eyes scanning his face for any sign of deceit. Slowly, she moved to the chair and sat, her body tense.

"How did you even get this far?" she asked, her tone sharp with skepticism. "How does someone like you end up here?"

Marcus hesitated, the weight of her question settling heavily on him. "It started with a murder," he said quietly.

Lila's expression changed, her wariness mingling with fear. "A murder?"

Marcus nodded. "A girl named Isabel. She was found in an alley, discarded like trash. No ID, no leads—just another victim they thought no one would care about. But I cared. I followed the trail, and it led me here."

The mention of Isabel's name caused Lila to stiffen. Her hands gripped the arms of the chair, her voice barely above a whisper. "Isabel…I knew her."

Marcus's chest tightened. "You did?"

Lila nodded slowly, her gaze distant. "She was at the warehouse. She was always scared. More than the rest of us. She couldn't…she couldn't fake it like they wanted her to. It made them angry."

"What happened to her?" Marcus asked, though he already feared the answer.

Lila's voice cracked. "One day, they took her and…" she hesitated for a moment, "we knew she wasn't coming back."

The silence that followed was oppressive. Marcus's fists clenched at his sides as he processed her words.

"I'm sorry, Lila," he said softly. "She didn't deserve that. None of you do."

Lila looked down, tears spilling onto her cheeks. "They'll kill me too," she whispered. "If they find out I talked to you…they'll kill me."

"They won't," Marcus said firmly. "But I need you to stay strong. Keep doing what you've been doing. Play your role, and follow their instructions. Don't draw attention to yourself. Can you do that?"

Lila hesitated, then nodded. "What about you? What if they find out about you?"

"They won't," Marcus said, his tone resolute. "My job is to stay ahead of them. And I will."

The faint sound of footsteps in the hallway made them both freeze. Lila's eyes widened in panic.

"Stay calm," Marcus whispered.

Before he could react, Lila bolted from her chair and moved toward him. Her movements were frantic, fueled by desperation. In one swift motion, she climbed onto his lap, her slender arms wrapping tightly around his neck. Before Marcus could react, she pressed her lips to his with a fervent urgency, her trembling body flush against his. Marcus's brain screamed in protest, and he froze for a split second, his arms instinctively hovering in the air, unsure of what to do. The faint scent of her perfume mixed with the panic in her shallow breaths. His heart pounded in his chest, and a surge of shock coursed through him.

Then he heard the doorknob turn.

The door opened, revealing the tall, broad-shouldered guard from earlier. His sharp gaze swept across the room, landing on Marcus and Lila in their seemingly intimate embrace. Marcus's brain raced to process the situation, the unexpected kiss still fresh on his lips. He forced himself to remain still, his instincts battling against the need to recoil. Instead, he did what Logan Harper would do.

He shifted in the chair slightly, leaning back as if indulging in the moment, his arm draping lazily around Lila's waist. He projected an air of satisfaction and control, masking the storm roiling inside him.

The guard tilted his head, his eyes narrowing as he took a step into the room. His gaze lingered on Lila, sharp and assessing, before shifting back to Marcus. "Everything all right in here, Mr. Harper? It's been awfully quiet."

Marcus forced a smirk, tilting his head to meet the man's gaze. "Everything's fine," he drawled, his tone calm and assured. "Just taking my time. Enjoying the moment."

The guard's eyes flicked back to Lila, his expression hardening slightly. "She looks a little… tense," he said, his tone measured. "Everything to your liking?"

Marcus's grip on Lila's waist tightened slightly, a subtle gesture of reassurance as he laughed softly, the sound casual and dismissive. "She was perfect," he said smoothly, "until you abruptly came in and startled her."

The guard blinked, his posture stiffening at the subtle shift in blame. Marcus leaned back further in the chair, exuding a relaxed confidence as he added, "Next time, maybe a knock or two."

Lila's breath hitched against his neck, her trembling more subdued now as she caught on to the cover story. Marcus's hand moved lightly along her back, selling the image of intimacy while maintaining his composure.

The guard's jaw tightened briefly, his expression unreadable as his eyes flicked between them one last time. "Understood," he said finally, his tone clipped. "I'm sorry, sir. Normally, the room isn't this…quiet. I thought I would check on you."

"Appreciate it," Marcus replied coolly, his smirk unwavering. "Now, unless there's something else, I'd rather not be interrupted again."

The guard hesitated for a moment, then gave a curt nod. "Enjoy your evening, sir." He stepped back and pulled the door shut behind him. The soft click of the lock echoed in the room.

As soon as the door closed, Lila pulled away from Marcus, stumbling back as tears streamed down her face. "I-I'm so sorry," she stammered, her voice trembling. "I didn't know what else to do. If he thought I wasn't…if he thought I wasn't doing my job—"

"Lila," Marcus interrupted gently, raising his hands in a calming gesture. "It's okay. You did what you had to do."

Her hands flew to her face as she backed against the wall. "I shouldn't have done that," she whispered, her voice cracking. "I just…I panicked."

Marcus rose slowly from the chair, keeping his movements measured. "You reacted the way anyone would in your position," he said firmly. "You protected yourself. Don't apologize for surviving."

Lila's sobs grew quieter, though her shoulders still shook with the effort of holding herself together. "They're always watching," she whispered. "Even when they're not in the room, I feel them watching. I can't…I can't do this anymore."

"You can," Marcus said, his voice steady. He stepped closer but stopped at a respectful distance away. "You've been surviving this long. You're stronger than you think."

She shook her head, her hands still trembling. "You don't know what it's like. The things they make us do…"

"I know more than you think," Marcus said softly. "But I promise you, Lila, I'm going to do everything I can to stop them. You're not alone anymore."

The room fell into a heavy silence, the weight of her reality pressing down on both of them. Finally, Marcus checked the time. "We need to make this look convincing before I leave," he said, his tone matter-of-fact.

Lila nodded, wiping her face with trembling hands. She moved to the mirror, fixing her hair and makeup as best as she could. Marcus loosened his tie further and unbuttoned the top few buttons of his shirt, ruffling his hair to complete the illusion of dishevelment. Every movement felt calculated, each one a small act of deception to ensure their survival.

As she smoothed her hair and dabbed at her tear-streaked cheeks, Marcus leaned against the desk, watching her closely. His thoughts churned with a mix of anger and sorrow, but he kept his voice steady as he broke the silence. "Lila…how old are you?"

Lila paused, her fingers stilling against her temple as she glanced at him warily. "I'm seventeen," she said quietly.

Marcus's chest tightened, but he nodded, keeping his expression calm.

When she turned back to him, she looked more composed, though the fear still lingered in her eyes. "Am I okay?" she asked hesitantly.

"You're perfect," Marcus said softly. "Just remember, you're not alone in this. Stay strong."

Her faint, trembling smile was the only response he needed. With a final nod, Marcus opened the door and stepped into the hallway. The guard from earlier stood nearby, his sharp eyes locking onto Marcus immediately.

"Everything to your satisfaction, Mr. Harper?" the guard asked, his tone polite but probing.

Marcus straightened his tie, allowing a faint smirk to curve his lips. "Absolutely. She's…a gem."

The guard nodded, his expression giving nothing away. "Safe travels, sir."

Marcus inclined his head and walked toward the elevator, his steps measured and deliberate. He could feel the guard's gaze on his back, but he didn't falter. When the elevator doors slid open, he stepped inside and let out a slow, controlled breath as they closed.

The descent felt endless, the mirrored walls reflecting the weight of the night etched into his face. By the time the elevator reached the lobby, Marcus had rebuilt his composure. He moved through the hotel's opulent entrance without a glance, stepping into the cool night air. He took a deep breath, forcing his feet to move toward the street.

He spotted Dana's car parked discreetly down the block, the faint glow of its dashboard light marking her presence. She'd been waiting, her watchful eyes likely scanning every passing car, every shadow. She was his anchor to the outside world, the one person who knew enough to help him carry the weight of this mission.

As he approached, his steps felt heavy, each one slower than the last. The events of the night replayed in his mind: Lila's trembling voice, her desperate kiss, the fear that radiated from her, and the way her words about Isabel had pierced through him like a blade.

When he reached the car, he hesitated, his hand hovering over the passenger-side door handle. For a moment, he considered turning back, retreating into the shadows. But there was no escape from the reality of what he had just experienced. With a sharp exhale, he opened the door and slid into the seat.

Dana turned toward him, her sharp eyes narrowing as they scanned his face. The tension in her posture was palpable, her hands gripping the steering wheel tightly. She looked like she'd been frozen in place since he'd gone inside, her nerves wound tight with anticipation.

"Well?" Dana's voice was steady but edged with urgency. "What happened in there?"

Marcus didn't meet her gaze. He stared straight ahead, his hands resting on his knees. The car's interior felt stifling despite the cool air seeping in from outside. For a long moment, the only sound was the faint hum of the car engine.

"Marcus," Dana pressed. "You have to tell me something. Did you get anything?"

He exhaled slowly, his shoulders slumping under the weight of the night. "Just drive," he said.

Dana frowned, her fingers tightening around the steering wheel. "No. You're not doing this again, Marcus," she said. "You can't just shut me out and expect me to pretend like nothing happened."

Marcus stared ahead. "Just drive," he said again.

The words struck Dana, causing her grip to loosen slightly. "You think this is easy for me?" she said, quieter now. "Sitting here, waiting, not knowing if you're walking out of that building alive? If you don't tell me anything, how am I supposed to help you?"

Marcus exhaled, shaking his head slightly. "I don't need your help. I just need you to drive."

The finality in his tone silenced her. Dana opened her mouth to argue again but stopped, her lips pressing into a thin line. With a sharp inhale, she started the car, her frustration evident in the way her fingers gripped the steering wheel. The tension between them sat heavy, unspoken but impossible to ignore.

They pulled away from the curb in silence. Marcus leaned back in his seat, tilting his head against the window. The passing city lights blurred into streaks of gold and white, their glow doing little to soothe the turmoil raging inside him. Dana stole glances at him as she drove. The silence between them grew heavier with each passing block.

"Marcus," she said gently, breaking the quiet. "Whatever it is, you don't have to carry it alone. You know that, right?"

Marcus closed his eyes briefly, his hand rubbing at his temple. "Not tonight," he said quietly, the exhaustion in his tone leaving no room for argument.

The car turned onto Marcus's street, the familiar surroundings offering a faint sense of relief. Dana pulled to the curb in front of his building and cut the engine. For a moment, neither of them moved, the silence between them heavy and unbroken.

Dana turned to him one last time, her voice calm but insistent. "Marcus…I get it. I do. But we're in this together, whether you like it or not. So when you're ready to talk, I'm here. Okay?"

Marcus reached for the door handle, pausing briefly. "Thanks," he said quietly, his voice steady but heavy with exhaustion. "Just…not tonight."

Dana nodded, though the worry in her eyes didn't fade. She watched as he stepped out of the car, her fingers tapping anxiously on the steering wheel. "Take care of yourself," she called after him.

Marcus didn't reply. He closed the door behind him and walked toward his building. The cold air brushed against his face, but it did little to clear the haze in his mind. At the door, he paused, glancing back at Dana's car before stepping inside.

Chapter 13

Marcus paced Elaine's living room with the restless energy of a caged animal, the scuff of his boots against the worn floor punctuating the heavy silence. Sunlight poured through the window, cutting through the dimness of the room but doing nothing to dispel the storm brewing inside him. His fists clenched and unclenched as he fought to wrangle the chaos of his thoughts into something coherent.

"I can't do this anymore," he growled. He turned sharply on his heel, his movements jerky and full of pent-up tension. "There has to be another way."

Elaine sat on the edge of her couch, her arms resting on her knees as her sharp eyes followed his restless movements.

"You're close, Marcus," she said. "Closer than you've ever been. After everything you've done, you can't stop now."

Marcus froze mid-step, spinning to face her. "I'm a 48-year-old man, Elaine!" he snapped, his voice rising with every word. "I just kissed a 17-year-old girl in a hotel room!"

Elaine arched an eyebrow, her expression unflinching. "Correction," she said evenly, her voice cutting through his outburst like a blade. "She kissed YOU. And if she hadn't, that guard may have blown your cover wide open."

Marcus barked a harsh laugh, bitter and hollow. He threw up his hands, his movements frantic. "That doesn't make it right!" he said, his voice breaking slightly. "It will never be right."

Elaine rose from the couch, crossing the room with deliberate steps until she was standing just a few feet away from him. Her voice softened, but her tone remained firm. "No, it's not right. None of this is. But you know what else isn't right? Walking away and leaving those girls behind because you can't handle your guilt."

He turned away from her, dragging a hand down his face as he stared out the window. His reflection stared back at him in the glass, distorted and fragmented. "You didn't see her, Elaine," he said, his voice thick with emotion. "You didn't see the fear in her eyes. The way she talked about the others in that warehouse…" His voice faltered, his throat tightening. "She's just a kid. And I left her there."

Elaine stepped closer. "She's already in it, Marcus," she said. "And she's not the only one. Do you think walking away will make things better for her? For any of them?"

"I'm not walking away," Marcus said sharply, spinning to face her again. His expression was raw, his eyes blazing with barely restrained anger. "But every second I don't act, it feels like I'm leaving her to suffer. Like I'm feeding her to the wolves."

Elaine's features softened slightly, though her tone remained resolute. "You're not feeding her to the wolves. You're building a way to take the wolves down. If you rush in now, you'll blow your cover, and then what? Everything you've done—all the risks you've taken—it'll mean nothing. And they'll win."

Marcus's hands curled into fists at his sides, his jaw clenched as her words sank in. His shoulders rose and fell with the effort of controlling his breathing. He knew she was right, but the truth didn't make it any easier to bear.

"What if I'm not enough?" he asked.

Elaine reached out, resting a steadying hand on his arm. "You're more than enough," she said firmly. "Because you care. That's what makes you different from them. And that's why you'll win."

He stared at her, her unwavering resolve grounding him even as doubt gnawed at his core. Slowly, he nodded, though the haunted look in his eyes didn't fade. He sank onto the couch, his elbows resting on his knees as he clasped his hands together. His thoughts churned like a storm, fragments of the past few weeks colliding with the weight of what he needed to do next.

Elaine's voice cut through his thoughts. "Marcus," she said. "You're overthinking. Whatever's bouncing around in your head, spit it out."

"I'm not overthinking," Marcus muttered. He leaned forward, his elbows digging into his knees as he met her gaze. "I'm figuring out how to get into that warehouse."

Elaine's stance softened slightly. "Go on," she said.

"There are premium girls," Marcus said. "Vince always brings one to the club—he shows them off, uses them to reel people in. If I tell him I want an upgrade—if I act like I'm willing to pay whatever it takes—he won't have a reason to keep them hidden from me."

Elaine's expression hardened, her skepticism clear. "You think he'll take you to them?"

Marcus nodded slowly. "He won't bring the whole lineup to the club. If I tell him I want to see my options, the only way for him to show me is to take me to where they're kept. To the warehouse."

Elaine stepped closer, crossing her arms. "And you're sure you can pull that off? That Vince won't see through you?"

"He trusts Logan Harper," Marcus said firmly. "I've spent weeks building this persona. Vince has seen me throw money around like it's nothing. He believes I'm someone who wants the best, someone who's willing to pay for exclusivity."

Elaine's eyes narrowed. "And what happens if he decides you're not who you say you are?"

Marcus hesitated, the weight of her question pressing against him. He exhaled slowly, his jaw tightening as he thought through the risks. "Then I adapt," he said finally. "That's what I've been doing since the start. I'll figure it out."

Elaine's gaze lingered on him, her expression unreadable. Finally, she gave a slight nod. "If you're going to do this, you better be ready. No hesitation. No second-guessing."

"I know," Marcus said quietly, though his voice carried the weight of the guilt and doubt still clinging to him.

"You say that," Elaine said, her voice softer now, "but last night shook you. I need to know you're not going to let it throw you off."

"This is the only way," he said softly, more to himself than to Elaine.

Elaine stepped forward and placed a firm hand on his shoulder, her voice steady and grounding. "Then focus on that," she said. "Forget everything else. Just get it done."

Marcus met her gaze, her unflinching resolve anchoring him. Slowly, he nodded, the glimmer of determination returning to his eyes. It was a dangerous plan, but it was the only way forward.

Chapter 14

The city's pulse thumped through the streets, neon lights flickering in a rhythm that felt almost alive. Marcus, buried deep in the persona of Logan Harper, sat in the passenger seat of an unmarked sedan parked a block from Vince Russo's exclusive club. As Logan, he felt both empowered and uneasy—a razor-thin balance between confidence in his crafted identity and the gnawing fear of being unmasked. The stakes, a precarious balance between life and death, had never been higher, and he knew one slip could mean the end, not just for him but for everything he'd been working toward.

Dana sat in the driver's seat, her fingers gripping the steering wheel tightly. She stole a glance at Marcus, her jaw tight with unease. Her voice broke the silence. "You're really going through with this?" she asked, her tone more accusatory than curious.

Marcus adjusted the cuff of his tailored jacket, his expression calm but resolute. "I've come too far to stop now. This is the only way we're going to get inside."

Dana exhaled sharply, shaking her head. "I don't like this, Marcus. It's too risky. Vince is dangerous, and if he even gets a whiff that you're not who you say you are…"

"He won't," Marcus interrupted, his tone steady. "Logan Harper is airtight."

Dana glanced toward the club, her brow furrowed. "Just be careful. Don't push too hard, too fast. These people don't play by any rules."

Marcus offered a faint smile, one that didn't reach his eyes. His mind was a whirlwind of conflicting emotions, his resolve warring with the fear of exposure. "I'll see you on the other side." He opened the door and stepped out, leaving Dana behind as he approached the club's imposing entrance.

Each step felt heavier than the last, a reminder of the perilous line he was walking. He could feel Dana's gaze lingering on him through the rearview mirror, her unspoken plea for his safety hanging in the air.

The bouncer at the door barely acknowledged Marcus's approach. With a curt nod, Marcus pulled the black card from his pocket and held it up.

"Mr. Harper," the bouncer said, his tone neutral as he stepped aside. The heavy door swung open, revealing the club's interior—a world of shadows, smoke, and indulgence.

The music hit him first—a low, throbbing bass that seemed to reverberate through his entire body. It rattled his composure for a moment, dragging him into the raw energy of the club. His pulse matched the beat, an unbidden rhythm of tension and anticipation. For a fleeting second, he wondered if his carefully constructed façade could withstand the weight of the atmosphere pressing down on him. The air was thick with smoke, the scent of expensive cigars mingling with the faint trace of exotic perfume. Velvet drapes lined the walls, and soft, amber lighting cast long shadows over the opulent decor. It was a place designed to overwhelm the senses, a playground for those who could afford to ignore morality.

He spotted Vince near the back, seated in a plush booth elevated slightly above the main floor. He was surrounded by his entourage, each member carefully selected to project wealth and power. A striking woman sat beside him, her presence deliberate and polished. She was a premium girl—Marcus could tell by her poise, her beauty, and the way she looked as though she might shatter under Vince's grip.

Marcus squared his shoulders and made his way toward the booth. His pulse quickened, but his expression remained unflinching. This was a test, and failure was not an option. Heads turned as he passed, some eyes curious, others wary. The Logan Harper persona had to be flawless tonight. When he reached the booth, Vince looked up, a smug smile spreading across his face. Marcus's jaw tightened, but he maintained his calm exterior.

"Logan Harper," Vince drawled, extending a hand. "Back so soon? How was your first taste of..." he paused for a moment as he recounted his memories, "Lila…was it?"

Marcus returned the handshake with practiced ease, his grip firm yet not overly strong. "The experience was unparalleled," he said smoothly, his voice dripping with the arrogance of someone used to getting what they wanted.

Vince's smile widened, though his eyes remained calculating. "Have a seat, Logan. So what's the occasion tonight?"

Marcus took a seat across from Vince. "I'm here because I want more," he said. "An…upgrade, you might say."

"Ah, I see," Vince said. "We definitely have upgrades." He gestured to the girl beside him. "This is Sasha. She's 19 but fresh. She's one of our finest. Tell me, Logan, does she meet your standards?"

Marcus noted how Sasha's smile wavered ever so slightly, the corners of her mouth unable to fully mask the tension in her jaw. Her hands, resting delicately on her lap, trembled just enough for someone paying attention to notice. He could see the flicker of fear in her eyes, a muted plea hidden behind the polished veneer she'd been forced to wear. It twisted something deep inside him, a sharp reminder of why he was here. Still, he maintained his detached demeanor, knowing that even the slightest crack in Logan Harper's persona could endanger not just himself but her as well.

Marcus let his gaze drift over Sasha, maintaining the detached interest of a man evaluating merchandise. He offered a small, polite smile before shaking his head. "She's stunning, but I'm looking for more of a pick-and-choose type of situation." His words were calm and composed, but inwardly, he felt the weight of leaving Sasha behind, unable to act in the moment. He had to remind himself that this was a long game, that saving her now could risk the entire operation. Still, the image of her subtle distress burned into his mind, fueling his determination to see this through.

Vince's eyebrows lifted slightly, and the men seated around him exchanged subtle glances. "Ambitious," Vince said, leaning back in his seat. He put his arm around Sasha and pulled her closer to him. "You sure you don't want this fiery beauty? She could be yours tonight for only $15,000."

"I don't believe in cutting corners," Marcus replied. "I believe everything has a price, and if the price is right, I'll bite. Especially if there was a lineup of all your finest…like Sasha here."

The atmosphere around the table shifted, the air thick with tension. Vince studied Marcus, his fingers tapping idly on the table. "You realize this isn't some department store, right? I can't just parade them out on a whim."

Marcus leaned forward, his smile sharp. "I'm not asking for a parade, Vince. I'm asking for an opportunity. Money's no object."

The room seemed to hold its breath as Vince considered him. Finally, he chuckled, though there was little humor in the sound. "You've got guts, Harper. I'll give you that."

Vince leaned closer, his voice lowering. "What you're asking for isn't handled by me. That's Nickoli's territory."

Marcus kept his expression neutral, though his pulse quickened. Nickoli. The name didn't sound familiar.

"Then let's arrange a meeting," Marcus said evenly. "I'd love to make his acquaintance."

Vince smirked. "Nickoli doesn't meet just anyone. You'll need to prove you're worth his time."

"I'm listening," Marcus said.

Vince gestured to a waiter, who brought over a sleek tablet. Vince tapped a few buttons before sliding it across the table to Marcus. "You said yourself, Logan...everything has a price."

Marcus looked down at the tablet. "Twenty-five thousand dollars, huh?"

"Non-refundable," Vince said with a toothy grin. "Think of it as your ticket to the show."

Marcus didn't flinch, pulling out his phone to initiate the wire transfer. The tablet pinged moments later, confirming the payment. Vince's grin widened. "Well, Harper, it seems you're serious after all."

Vince leaned back, signaling to the waiter again. "If Nickoli's interested, you'll get word. It could be a day or a week. Just be ready when the call comes."

"I'll be ready," Marcus replied.

Vince leaned forward again, his eyes locking onto Marcus. "Money may talk, Harper. But remember, Nickoli doesn't play around with it."

"Neither do I," Marcus replied, his tone cold enough to match Vince's. "I'm just looking for a good time with the best you've got."

The two men locked eyes for a moment before Vince broke into a laugh. "I like you, Harper," he said. "You've got the kind of edge that gets things done."

As Marcus stood to leave, Vince gestured to Sasha. "Let me at least send you off with a drink. On the house."

Marcus hesitated, but only briefly. "Appreciated," he said, taking the glass Sasha handed him. He raised it slightly before setting it down, untouched. "But I never drink before business."

Vince watched him with interest, nodding slowly. "Smart man."

Marcus stepped out of the club into the cool night air, his mind racing. A block away, Dana's car idled where he had left it. He walked briskly, slipping into the passenger seat as Dana's sharp eyes scanned him.

"Well?" she demanded, her voice clipped.

"There might be a meeting," Marcus said. "If I'm lucky, I'll get an invitation to meet Nickoli."

Dana raised an eyebrow. "Nickoli?"

"New name," Marcus said. "If this goes well, he'll take me to the warehouse."

Dana's eyes narrowed. "And if it doesn't?"

Marcus's expression hardened. "Then we're back to square one. But this is our best shot."

Dana exhaled sharply, shaking her head. "Just don't get yourself killed, Marcus. We're no good to anyone if this blows up."

Marcus offered her a faint smile. "I'll see it through." For a brief moment, doubt flickered in his mind—a whisper of uncertainty about the risks he was taking. But he pushed it aside, steeling himself with the reminder that failure wasn't an option.

Chapter 15

Marcus sat in the precinct's dimly lit briefing room, elbows on the table, fingers steepled beneath his chin. A file folder lay untouched in front of him, its corners slightly bent, a small detail that irritated him more than it should have. Overhead, the clock ticked with slow deliberation, filling the silence between them with a mechanical persistence.

Across the table, Dana leaned back in her chair, her arms crossed and jaw tight. The early hour had done nothing to dull the sharpness in her eyes. She glanced at the door, then back at Marcus.

"He didn't say what it was about?" she asked.

Marcus shook his head. "Only that it was urgent. Something tied to Elite Opportunities."

Dana let out a long breath, her gaze still fixed on the door. "God, I hope it's not another dead end."

Before Marcus could respond, the door creaked open. Nash stepped inside, a clipboard tucked beneath one arm, his expression carved from stone. He closed the door behind him without a word and remained standing, his presence commanding immediate attention.

"Thanks for coming in early," Nash began, eyes sweeping across both detectives. His voice was quiet, yet it held a gravity that made the air feel heavier. "I got a call this morning. Came through a federal liaison who occasionally updates us on overlapping jurisdictional activity. There's been a breach. One of their safehouses was compromised overnight. Two girls were taken."

Marcus sat up straighter. "What safehouse?"

"East side," Nash replied. "It's a quiet neighborhood. Residential. The house was being used to shelter two young girls, victims tied directly to Elite Opportunities. Their identities were classified. Only a select few even knew where they were."

Dana turned to Marcus, their eyes meeting. No words were exchanged. They didn't have to say it aloud.

"I want the two of you on this immediately," Nash continued. "You're already deep into the case. If there's any chance of recovering those girls, it starts with you two."

Marcus nodded once. "We'll find them."

"Keep this close," Nash said. "I want every detail vetted. No leaks. No whispers around the precinct. Anything you find comes directly to me. Understood?"

"Understood," Dana replied.

With a final nod, Nash turned and walked out, the soft click of the door closing behind him, leaving behind a silence that seemed to swell.

Dana looked at Marcus, frustration in her eyes. "This is getting out of hand. First the alias, now this? We need to bring Nash into the circle. He has a right to know what's really going on."

Marcus shook his head. "No. Not yet."

"Marcus...Jenna and Maya were kidnapped. That's not something you handle in the shadows. If we screw this up…"

" I know what's at stake," he said, cutting her off. "I'm close to Nickoli. Closer than anyone's ever been. If Nash knows, he'll involve the task force. Harper will be burned the moment anyone whispers his name inside the precinct."

Dana leaned forward, planting her hands on the table. "And if something happens to you? If you disappear and no one even knows what you were doing?"

Marcus met her gaze. "Then you take what I've left behind and burn them to the ground. All of them."

* * *

Later that night, Marcus sat in the dim quiet of his apartment, elbows resting on his knees as he stared through the cracked window. The low hum of the city drifted in—cars rolling through intersections, a distant horn, the faint rumble of the subway deep underground. The room around him felt hollow, stripped down to shadows and silence. He held his phone to his ear, unmoving.

"I heard," Dr. Lorraine Ford said on the other end, her voice rough, like it had been dragged across gravel.

Marcus closed his eyes, jaw clenched. "I'm sorry."

"Don't be sorry," she snapped, sharper than she likely meant to be. Then her tone dropped, brittle. "Just find them. Please."

"I will," he said. "I promise."

A pause stretched between them. Then Ford's voice returned, quieter now, edges dulled by exhaustion. "They were fine when I left them the night before. Jenna made cocoa. Maya stayed up sketching in her journal. It felt like they were starting to breathe again, you know? Then they were just...gone."

Marcus stared down at the floor, eyes distant. "I was careful when I visited. It was off record. I waited, doubled back, and made sure I wasn't followed. No one saw me."

"Then how did they know where to go?" she asked. "How did they find them?"

"I don't know," he said, voice low. "But someone does."

The silence that followed wasn't just grief—it was suspicion. It was the weight of something too big to track.

"There might be a leak," Marcus added. "Someone is bleeding information. That's why I'm keeping this even tighter now."

Her breath wavered. "Just bring them back, Marcus."

He looked out the window, his own reflection faint against the night. "I'll do everything I can."

The call ended without another word. Marcus lowered the phone to the table. His hand hovered there for a moment before pulling away. Outside, a siren rose and faded. Somewhere below, a motorcycle tore through the streets. In here, there was nothing but stillness.

Then the phone buzzed again, rattling once across the table. He stared at it, his chest tightening as something cold crawled along his spine.

After a brief pause, he answered. "Yeah?"

There was no immediate reply. Just a breath, subtle and deliberate. Then came the voice, with an unmistakable European accent. "Logan Harper."

Marcus straightened in his chair. "Speaking."

The pause that followed wasn't hesitation—it was control. "You made an impression," the voice said.

"Nickoli?" Marcus asked.

"Vince speaks highly of you," the voice continued, each word clean and surgically precise. "He tells me you're ready for more."

Marcus kept his response clipped. "I am."

"Then consider this your invitation," the voice said. "When the time is right, I'll contact you with a location."

Another pause. Then the line went dead. Marcus stayed where he was, the phone still in his hand. The apartment was silent again, but everything had shifted. The board was in motion, and he was officially in play.

Chapter 16

The rain came down in sheets, drowning the city in a cold, relentless haze. Marcus stood beneath the overhang outside the precinct, collar up, coffee forgotten in his hand. The storm wasn't just in the sky tonight. It had settled in his chest and hadn't let up since Nickoli's voice rasped through his phone. He hadn't slept. Not really. Just drifted in and out, eyes open, heart pacing like a drum.

He was still staring into the murky dark when Dana pulled up in her cruiser, her headlights slicing through the rain. She didn't get out. Just leaned over and popped the passenger-side door. Marcus climbed in without a word.

"We got something," Dana said, keeping her eyes on the road as she pulled away. "Patrol picked up a body dumped behind a textile plant off Merritt Street. Female. Early twenties. But..." She didn't finish. Marcus didn't ask her to.

The silence stretched, thick and raw. Marcus stared out the window, rain carving jagged lines down the glass. He already knew. He felt it deep in his gut.

The textile plant sat at the edge of the industrial zone, surrounded by rusted fences and long-forgotten machinery. A single patrol car lit the alleyway in strobing red and blue, and a uniformed officer stood under a tarp, nodding grimly as Marcus and Dana approached.

She lay curled near a dumpster, half-covered by a torn plastic sheet. Her body was twisted, knees drawn up, arms folded tight to her chest as if she'd tried to make herself smaller. Her skin was pale, her lips tinged blue, and her hair soaked dark with rain. But it was the necklace that confirmed it. A thin silver chain with a single glass charm. Jenna had worn it during the meeting. She had a nervous tic, constantly fidgeting with it when she spoke about the warehouse. About the monsters that paraded her around like a commodity.

Dana knelt beside the body. "We'll need to wait for Hunt to make it official, but I'm calling it now."

Marcus didn't answer. He couldn't. Something heavy closed around his throat. There was blood. Not a lot, but enough. Around the mouth. Under the nails. Bruising along her wrists and her throat. Not quick. Not clean.

"She fought," Dana said quietly.

Marcus nodded. "Of course she did."

He stepped back, his jaw clenched, fists trembling at his sides. The alley swam in and out of focus. Jenna's broken form was burned behind his eyes, even when he looked away. She had escaped hell. Trusted them. Trusted him. And now she was on the ground, discarded like garbage. He should've done more.

Dana stood, brushing rain from her sleeves, watching him carefully. "You're not responsible for this, Marcus."

"The hell I'm not," he replied.

"You didn't put her there," Dana said.

"No," he said, voice sharp with self-recrimination. "But I left her unprotected. I let myself believe we were ahead of them. That I was still in control. I should have done more. I should have been there for her."

Dana didn't argue. There was nothing she could say that would pull him out of it. So she gave him space. They waited until Lorraine Hunt arrived, soaked and stone-faced beneath her forensic gear. She examined the body with her usual quiet precision, cataloging each injury with clipped efficiency. But even Lorraine, seasoned and clinical, paused a beat longer than usual as she gently removed the necklace.

"Time of death?" Dana asked.

"Hard to say exactly," Hunt replied. "But she's been dead less than twenty-four hours. Bruising, ligature marks, evidence of restraint. I'll have more after the autopsy."

Marcus turned to go.

"Where are you headed?" Dana called after him.

"Elaine," he said.

* * *

Elaine's apartment was dim, lit only by the bluish glow of her laptop screens and the low flicker of a candle burning beside a stack of notes. She looked up as Marcus stepped in, her eyes wide the moment she saw his face.

"Who?" she asked.

"Jenna," Marcus said, closing the door behind him.

Elaine covered her mouth with one hand.

"They found her behind a textile mill," he continued, voice low and flat. "Dumped in the rain. Just like Isabel."

Elaine sank into her chair, hands trembling as she reached for the edge of the table. "Marcus, I..."

He sat across from her, elbows on his knees, staring at nothing. "We failed her."

Elaine looked at him, eyes rimmed with tears. "You did everything you could."

Marcus shook his head slowly. "No. I waited. I played by their rules. I told myself it was the only way in. But while I was playing the part of Logan Harper, she was being dragged back into hell."

Elaine leaned forward, her voice fierce despite the pain. "You didn't kill Jenna. Nickoli did. Vince did. The men who built this system did. You want to blame yourself? Fine. But don't forget who you're really fighting."

Marcus met her gaze. It was the fire in her eyes that steadied him.

"Then help me stop them," he said.

Elaine nodded, wiping at her eyes. "We have to assume they moved Maya, too. Maybe not back to the same place, but somewhere close. If they felt the walls closing in, they wouldn't scatter. They'd consolidate. Pull in tighter."

Marcus rubbed a hand over his face. "Which means the warehouse."

"It has to be," Elaine said.

He looked around her workspace—the maps, the pinned photos, the red thread of a war board that rivaled the precinct.

"What do you need from me?" Elaine asked.

"Keep digging. Anything you can find on their property holdings. Storage spaces. Commercial fronts. Even old utility hookups. We need to predict where they'll take me."

Elaine nodded. "And what about Nickoli?"

Marcus's voice turned to stone. "He'll call again. When he does, I'll be ready."

* * *

That night, Marcus stood by his window, staring out into the street below. Rain continued to fall, now softer, more like a whisper than a scream. He hadn't turned the lights on. The room felt too heavy for it.

Jenna's face hovered in his mind. That first day, she hadn't trusted him. Who could blame her? But slowly, she had. She'd risked everything just by speaking. And now she was gone. He pulled out his notebook and opened it to a fresh page. At the top, he wrote her name. Jenna Clarke.

He listed everything they knew. Last seen at the safehouse on the east side, around 10:45 PM. Then he turned the page and wrote another name. Maya Lopez.

He stared at the names until the ink began to blur. Somewhere in the dark, Nickoli was watching. Jenna was dead. Maya might still be alive—barely. Not because of mercy. But because she was still valuable. And Marcus Cole was out of patience.

Chapter 17

The car was silent as it moved through the city. Vince Russo sat behind the wheel like he owned the night. Marcus Cole—Logan Harper to everyone who mattered now—sat beside him, expression unreadable, nerves buried deep under layers of cultivated poise.

"You're quiet tonight," Vince said, making a lazy turn off the main road. The city lights began to thin behind them, swallowed by the industrial sprawl. "Nervous, Harper?"

Marcus smirked faintly, shifting in his seat. "Cautious. You said Nickoli doesn't waste his time. I figure I shouldn't waste mine either."

Vince gave a low chuckle, eyes on the road. "Good instinct. But be careful what you say around him. Nickoli's the kind of guy who listens harder to what you don't say. Silence is its own language."

The road narrowed, buildings giving way to warehouses and razor-wire fences. The air changed—denser, colder, like something old and buried still lingered here. Fog from the nearby canal curled low along the ground, the mist clinging to the base of the fencing like a ghost unsure of where to rest.

"This is it," Vince murmured as he pulled off onto a side road. A steel gate loomed ahead. Without slowing, he flicked his headlights twice. It creaked open as if on cue. Marcus caught sight of two guards in heavy coats and earpieces. Neither looked at the car as it passed. The warehouse loomed, a behemoth of concrete and shadow. No signage. No lights in the upper windows. Just a single, buzzing lamp above the side entrance. Vince parked beside the door and turned off the engine. Silence pressed in.

"Ready?" he asked, glancing over.

Marcus nodded once. "Always."

Inside, the air was dry and cold. The lighting was low, industrial, humming with fluorescent fatigue. The scent of bleach clung faintly beneath everything else, sterile and unnerving. A narrow hallway stretched ahead of them, dim and windowless. It opened into a cavernous interior—the rotation floor. Girls sat on couches against the far wall, backs straight, eyes down. Each of them dressed similarly, with subtly different shades of soft tones. They looked like mannequins.

Men lingered nearby; some seated with drinks, while others stood in pairs, chatting softly. Laughter cracked the silence here and there. Not joyous laughter. Empty. Possessive. Guards stood at every exit. Stone-faced and alert.

Vince walked down the center aisle with the air of a king inspecting his court. Marcus followed, gaze detached, noting everything—the layout, the faces, the doors.

"Recognize anyone?" Vince asked casually, a smug curl at the corner of his mouth.

Marcus didn't answer at first. His gaze had already landed on her. Lila. She stood near the far end, partially behind a divider. Her dark hair had been curled, her lips painted a deep, soft pink. But it was her eyes that caught him—wide, watchful, brimming with a flicker of fear. She saw him. Recognition passed between them like a current. And then she looked away.

"You remember her, don't you?" Vince said. "Lila. She was your first."

Marcus nodded, forcing a smirk. "Hard to forget."

"She's held up well," Vince remarked, his tone clinical. "But tonight's not about reminiscing. Come on."

They moved past the rotation floor to a guarded door. Vince produced a card and passed it under a scanner. A soft buzz and the door opened. The corridor on the other side was cleaner and quieter. More sterile. The doors at the end opened into a luxurious lounge, stark in its elegance. White marble floors. Black leather chairs. Silver fixtures that gleamed like surgical instruments. A single fireplace flickered cold blue against a mirrored wall.

A man stood at the far end, his back to them, studying a wall display of imported wines.

"Mr. Harper," the man said without turning. "We finally meet."

He turned slowly. Pale gray eyes that didn't blink. Hair slicked immaculately to the side. Every movement calculated and deliberate. Nickoli. He approached without a rush, circling a chair between them like a predator studying a guest.

"You've made an impression on Vince," Nickoli said. "That's no small feat."

Marcus kept his posture relaxed and his voice cool. "I value discretion. Vince values results. I provide both."

Nickoli chuckled. "You understand the language of this world. That's good. But understand this: money gets you through the door. Loyalty keeps you breathing."

He gestured to a curtain off to the side. "You asked for the premium experience. Shall we?" A nod from Nickoli and an attendant swept the curtain aside.

Marcus stepped through. His breath caught. Five girls stood in a polished, windowless room. Spotlit from above. Dressed in shades of pale blush and silver. Their makeup was immaculate. Their expressions were hollow. But Marcus saw only one.

Maya.

She stood third from the left. And when she saw him—really saw him—she flinched. Then her eyes widened. Shock. Recognition. Confusion. Then something else. Hope.

Marcus didn't allow himself more than a glance. He gave a slow, approving nod, then gestured with a flick of his hand.

"Her."

Nickoli's voice followed from behind. "She's one of our more...difficult ones."

Marcus kept his tone level. "She'll learn."

Nickoli stepped into his peripheral vision, his eyes sharp.

"I'll have the Regency set up for Friday night. Suite 209. One night. You'll be observed. If you pass, the door stays open."

Marcus nodded once, keeping his tone even. "Understood."

Nickoli studied him a moment longer, eyes assessing, then gave a slight nod. He turned and exited through the far door without another word.

A beat later, Vince appeared at Marcus's side. "This way."

They retraced their steps in silence. Marcus was halfway to the car when something caught his eye. A second-floor balcony overlooked the warehouse floor. There, under soft lighting, stood a man in a dark coat, speaking with one of the guards. Chief Gregory Nash.

Marcus froze. Nash didn't look down. He was engaged in conversation, hands folded behind his back, expression calm. But Marcus saw him. Saw enough. He swallowed hard. His pulse surged. Every puzzle piece clicked into place. The leak. Jenna. The chief. The damn chief.

Vince had already unlocked the car. "Something wrong?"

Marcus shook his head quickly and climbed in. "Just processing."

The ride back was a blur. Vince said nothing. Neither did Marcus. The city lights returned. The fog lifted. But Marcus's thoughts were buried miles away. When Vince dropped him off, Marcus stood outside for a long moment, letting the wind rake over him. He could still see Nash's face. Still hear Jenna's voice. Still feel the weight of Maya's stare.

He moved quickly, covering the final few blocks to his apartment in just minutes. Once inside, he pulled out his phone and began dialing.

* * *

Elaine and Dana arrived twenty minutes later. Marcus opened the door without a word and pointed them to the kitchen.

"It's Nash," he said finally. "I saw him tonight. At the warehouse. Talking to one of Nickoli's guards. He didn't see me. But I saw him."

Elaine stared. Dana blinked slowly.

"You're sure?" Dana asked.

"I'd bet my life," Marcus replied.

Dana sank into a chair, pale. "The timing. The access to safehouse intel. Jenna."

Elaine said nothing at first. She looked down at her hands, then back at Marcus. "If it really is him, then we can't go through normal channels. He'll kill this investigation before it ever reaches Nickoli."

Marcus nodded slowly. "Which means I'm in this alone. At least until we have proof."

Dana exhaled hard. "Then we better get it fast."

Elaine opened her laptop and began typing. "Let me see what I can pull on Nash's off-hours movement. His financials. I'll find something."

Marcus sat down, the chair creaking beneath him. "Tomorrow night, I meet Maya at the Regency. Nickoli made it clear that I'll be watched. But it's our best shot at getting her out."

Elaine looked up. "Can you pull this off without blowing your cover?"

"I think so," he said.

Dana met his gaze. "You sure you're ready for that?"

Marcus didn't hesitate. "I have to be."

Outside, the city moved on, oblivious to the events. But inside Marcus's apartment, the lines had been drawn. The war had turned personal. And now, everything depended on what came next.

Chapter 18

The rain came in light drizzles that morning, casting a gray veil across the city skyline. Marcus barely felt it as he stepped out of his car, jaw clenched and heart beating faster than he wanted to admit. Dana matched his stride, her pace sharp, shoulders stiff with restrained energy. They crossed the precinct lobby without a word, ignoring greetings and sidelong glances.

When they reached Chief Nash's office, Marcus didn't knock. He pushed the door open and walked in. Nash was at his desk, reading over a file. He looked up, neither startled nor surprised. Just waiting.

"We need to talk," Marcus said, his voice hard.

Dana closed the door behind them and stepped forward. "Privately," she said.

Nash studied them for a moment, then calmly reached for the blinds, drawing them closed one by one. The slats shut with a rhythmic clack. He turned the lock on the office door and returned to his seat, folding his hands across his desk.

"Well?" he asked.

"I saw you," Marcus said, stepping closer. "At the warehouse. Second-floor balcony. You were talking to one of Nickoli's guards."

Dana's eyes were cold steel. "You want to explain that, Chief?"

Nash didn't flinch. In fact, he let a small, dry smile form at the corners of his mouth. He tilted his head slightly and then, in a voice laced with something just shy of amusement, said: "And what about you, Logan?"

The silence in the room thickened. Marcus's eyes narrowed. Dana blinked.

"What did you just say?" Marcus asked, though he already knew.

"You think I didn't recognize you at the gala?" Nash replied. "Expensive suit. Perfectly rehearsed alias. Access no street-level detective could buy." He leaned back in his chair. "You weren't the only one undercover that night."

Marcus stood frozen.

"I've known about Logan Harper since the moment you stepped onto the ballroom floor," Nash continued. "Had to make sure your name didn't end up on any real watchlists. The fact that Nickoli didn't sniff you out told me you were good. Real good."

"Then why not pull me out?" Marcus asked, voice low.

"Because by the time I confirmed it was you, you were already too deep," Nash said. "If I pulled you, I would've exposed myself and killed your access. So I let Harper live."

Dana crossed her arms, still trying to process. "You knew the whole time?"

"I suspected. Confirmed it by the end of the gala," Nash said. "And I knew better than to interfere with a working cover. Especially one this risky."

Marcus exhaled slowly. The pieces were shifting again.

"So let me guess," Marcus said. "You being at the warehouse...that wasn't betrayal."

"No," Nash replied. "It was surveillance. I've been embedded in a federal task force—off the books. Deep infiltration. My assignment wasn't to make arrests. It was to trace the network upward."

He reached into a drawer and pulled out a black folder. He opened it and turned it toward them—photos, intercepted communications, and a sealed document marked DOJ CONFIDENTIAL.

"I've been watching this network for over a year," he said. "Judges, city officials, foreign financiers. The people pulling the strings are so far up the ladder they don't even know what street-level trafficking looks like anymore."

Marcus flipped through the contents. Dana leaned in silently, eyes scanning the evidence.

Nash continued. "I didn't tell anyone. Not even you two. Because the moment anyone breathes a word wrong in this department, the news spreads. You've seen how fast they move when they're tipped off."

"You saw Nickoli face-to-face?" Dana asked.

"Twice," Nash confirmed. "Long enough to convince him I was someone with reach. Someone who belonged. Long enough to hear whispers about Harper."

Dana nodded." So when Marcus showed up in the rotation?"

Nash gave a tight smile. "I knew he'd beaten me to the inner circle. You got deeper than I ever could."

Marcus shook his head. "What about Jenna and Maya?" he asked. "If you didn't leak their location, then who did?"

Nash shrugged his shoulders. "I'm still trying to figure that one out."

There was a long silence, the gravity of it settling between them. Then Nash leaned forward, folding his hands. "Now let me say this plain and clear—what you two did, going rogue, risking your careers, it was reckless. I would also say foolish."

Dana straightened, about to fire back, but Nash cut her off with a raised hand. "But it was also brave as hell. I wish I could tell you to stand down. I wish I could pull you both off this and keep you safe. But it's too late. Harper's in too deep, and this network's already reacting. If you back out now, everything we've built collapses."

Marcus met his eyes. "Then we finish it."

Nash gave a slow nod. "We finish it. But understand this, Marcus. You're walking a line you haven't been fully trained for. When this is over—if it works—I don't know if you're looking at a promotion...or termination."

Dana gave a bitter smile. "That's comforting."

"It's honest," Nash said. "And right now, that's all I've got."

Marcus nodded. "Then let's get to work."

They moved to a windowless municipal building just south of the river—an old zoning office turned dead site. The kind of place that had been forgotten by the city and never missed. Concrete walls. Fluorescent lights hummed overhead. Dust still clung to the corners of the ceiling. A metal door, secured with a keypad and chain, kept out anyone who didn't know the code.

Inside, the walls were bare, but the table was full of maps, schematics, and field reports. The air smelled faintly of printer ink and stale coffee.

Nash took position at the head of the room, a tablet in one hand and a black folder in the other. He'd been operating out of this place for months, running silent surveillance ops through federal drop points and burner phones. It had the feel of a war room now—controlled chaos anchored by hard decisions.

Elaine Monroe arrived within minutes, her laptop already open before she found a seat. Her hair was pulled back, her eyes sharp. She didn't need instruction —within seconds, she was connected to hotel blueprints, precinct backchannels, and a suite of encrypted feeds only a hacker of her caliber could summon. She moved with the coolness of someone who lived in two worlds—the real one and the digital one behind it.

"Let's start with the warehouse," Nash said, spreading out the first schematic. The blueprint was old, but it had been updated in red ink, highlighting entry points and blind spots. He pointed to the rotation floor. "We breach here. Two teams. Simultaneous entry from the east and south wings. We sweep in through these corridors and converge here."

He marked a central access point between the staging floor and the loading dock.

"Dana, you'll take point on the west team. You're extraction. Your job is to clear the floor and get those girls out."

Dana nodded, arms folded tightly across her chest. "What about fire teams?"

"They'll be with you," Nash replied. "Three-man sweep teams. Staggered intervals. We minimize exposure and maximize clearance. No radio chatter once we move in. Secure comms only."

"SWAT?" she asked.

"I've already got them briefed," Nash said. "They're out of the 17th. I handpicked the unit's lead myself—

he's burned operations with ICE and DEA. Nobody in our precinct knows. No chatter. No risk."

Elaine turned her laptop toward them, her screen split into four quadrants—each feed running real-time test footage from the Regency Hotel. Hallways. Elevators. Parking garage.

"I've backdoored the hotel's surveillance," she said, tapping keys as she typed. "We'll have a live feed of every camera inside. I've mapped the loop schedule. There's a thirty-eight-second blind spot on the second-floor west stairwell every twelve minutes. That's our rhythm."

Marcus stood at the corner of the table, staring at the floor plan of the hotel. Suite 209. Second floor. One window. One bathroom. One door. One shot.

"She'll be watched," Marcus said, eyes locked on the blueprint. "They'll probably have at least one guard outside the room, maybe one posted down the hall."

Nash nodded. "We assume worst-case. Everything you do in there has to be under control."

"She'll be scared," Marcus added. "She'll recognize me, but she'll also know we're being watched."

"You'll have to walk the line," Dana said. "Play the role, but tip her off. Get her ready."

"What's the plan for extraction?" Marcus asked.

Nash tapped a section of the blueprint near the window. "There's a two-man rescue team staged under the tree line across from the hotel's rear alley. Unmarked van, infrared gear, silent comms. Maya goes out the window. The team extracts and disappears in ninety seconds or less."

"And me?" Marcus asked.

"Turn the shower on and walk out," Dana said. "Logan Harper doesn't panic. He doesn't bolt. You had a nice evening with Maya. She hops in the shower, and you walk out. Or so the guard thinks. You keep your cover until the last possible second."

Nash looked up from the table, meeting his eyes. "Just don't get yourself killed. We've got enough bodies tied to this thing."

There was a moment of silence as they scanned over the blueprints again before Nash looked up from his tablet. "I've got a question."

Marcus met his gaze.

Nash gestured vaguely. "How'd you pull it off? The buy-ins, the transfers? Nickoli's ring isn't cheap."

Marcus was quiet for a moment, then said, "Combination of untraceable cash. Some skimmed from civil forfeiture money that was about to be incinerated.

And an old FBI contingency fund a friend helped us route through. Quiet and clean."

Nash raised a brow. "Elaine?"

Elaine smirked. "You're welcome."

Nash chuckled. "Creative. Dangerous as hell. But creative."

He turned to Marcus. He studied him a moment longer. The silence wasn't uncomfortable—it was measured. "You played your part better than most feds I've worked with."

Marcus met his eyes. "We're not the same."

"No," Nash agreed. "But we're in the same fire now."

He stepped closer, lowering his voice. "If this works, you'll have burned one of the most dangerous trafficking networks on the eastern seaboard. You'll have walked through the fire and out the other side."

"And if it doesn't work?" Marcus asked.

Nash gave the faintest of smiles. "Then you'll disappear under the weight of this op, and no one will ever hear about Logan Harper again."

Marcus nodded once. "Understood."

As they packed up, Elaine lingered a second longer. "You think we're ready?" she asked quietly.

"No," Marcus said. "But we're committed."

He stepped outside into the cold, rainy weather. The sky was the color of gunmetal, the street slick with oil and water. His coat flapped behind him in the wind as he paused on the steps, staring out toward the shadowed city skyline.

Somewhere out there, Maya waited. Somewhere out there, Nickoli and Vince were still trying to hold their empire together. But they were coming. And this time, there were no more secrets.

Chapter 19

Marcus walked across the lobby of the Regency Hotel. The elevator doors opened with a quiet chime. Two men stood near them, dressed in tailored suits that failed to hide their purpose. One of them glanced at Marcus. The nod they exchanged was subtle but enough. Surveillance was active. Nickoli's men were watching.

Marcus stepped into the elevator, turned to face the doors, and adjusted his cufflinks with a calm he didn't feel. The polished metal reflected his own eyes back at him, flat and unreadable. Floor two. Suite 209. The hallway was quiet. Too quiet, the carpet muting his steps. He stopped in front of the door and knocked once. It opened after a beat. Maya stood on the other side.

Her face was pale, her cheek bruised, and her lips chapped. She wore a silk robe, cinched tight, her arms folded as if bracing for impact. But her eyes met his without hesitation.

"You picked me," she said quietly. "At the warehouse. Why me?"

Marcus stepped in and closed the door behind him. "Because you already know who I am," he replied as he looked around the room, scanning the corners for camera lenses. "And your trust in me will help this operation go smoothly."

"Operation?" Maya asked, voice low.

"I'm here to get you out," Marcus said. "There is a raid going on at the warehouse right now. We're going to get all of you girls out."

A flicker of hope flashed across her face. Fragile but present. She took a slow breath, then stepped away from the door, glancing at the drawn curtains. Her hands trembled slightly. Marcus moved to the small round table near the window, pulled out the chair, and sat down. The room was elegantly furnished, featuring a king-sized bed, ornate light fixtures, and a tray of untouched wine and strawberries. He could feel the surveillance even if he couldn't see it.

Maya remained by the window, chewing the inside of her cheek. "They said you were a buyer. A high-tier one. That Nickoli had plans for you."

"It was the only way in," Marcus said. "I paid, yes. But every move I made was to get closer to this moment."

She nodded slowly, believing him. Maya had survived worse. She knew how to read danger. And she saw none in him. "There's something else," she said. "When they took me and Jenna from the safehouse...one of them didn't have a mask. It was dark, but I think I recognized her."

Marcus went still. "Her?"

Maya nodded. "There were two men who broke in. The woman...she didn't come inside. She was waiting in the car. But I saw her when they pushed us out to the trunk. Just for a second. She used to visit the center after I was rescued. We all knew her as Marisol. But that night...she was one of them."

Marisol.

The name landed like a stone. Marcus reached beneath the table and tapped his watch—three short pulses.

"We'll deal with that later," he said, eyes scanning hers. "Right now, you follow my lead. Everything depends on that."

She nodded. "Tell me what to do."

He glanced toward the window. "When I signal, you climb out. There is a team down below. They will catch you. There will be a van waiting across the alley. They'll pull you in and vanish. No noise. No mistakes."

"And you?" she asked.

"I walk out," Marucs replied. "Just another client after a night of luxury."

She nodded, "Let's do it."

* * *

Across the city, the storm began. At 11:03 p.m., the steel doors of the warehouse blew inward with the thunderclap of a breaching charge. Smoke grenades hissed along the ground, curling white tendrils into the shadows. Red laser sights cut through the haze as flashbangs detonated in sharp bursts, each one a burst of light and noise that disoriented everyone inside.

Dana moved like a bullet through the chaos, rifle shouldered, night-vision goggles down tight. The strike team from the 17th Precinct was right behind her, two squads advancing in staggered waves, precise and fluid.

"Left flank! Hostile!" someone called out.

Dana pivoted, dropped to one knee, and squeezed the trigger. The man dropped instantly, his body crumpling against the wall in a heap of limbs.

"Clear!"

They pressed forward into the rotation floor—a cavernous expanse of concrete and rebar lit by flickering overheads. Girls were huddled in corners, some locked behind fencing, others forced into alcoves meant for livestock.

"Move! Move! Get them out of there!"

Dana slung her rifle and rushed to the nearest enclosure. Her voice was calm but forceful.

"You're safe now," she said. "Come with me. Quickly."

Three girls stumbled forward—one crying, one limping, the third clutching another girl by the hand as they crossed into the chaos of freedom.

Across the compound, Chief Gregory Nash led Team Two through the premium wing. His sidearm was raised, his steps measured. The comm in his ear crackled.

"West stairwell secure. Hall two breached."

He advanced down the corridor, clearing doors one by one with his team moving in a diamond formation behind him. They reached the final suite, executive level.

Nash stepped aside as an officer wedged open the security door with a hydraulic spreader. Inside, on the desk, sat a laptop, its screen still glowing.

"Got something!" a voice called out.

Nash crossed the room and narrowed his eyes. A command prompt was running, lines of code streaming by. A digital wipe—already in progress.

"Nickoli," Nash muttered.

He yanked the power cable and handed the machine to the waiting tech. "Kill the feed. Scrape everything. I want it all."

Down the hall, an officer's voice came through the comm. "We've got Russo! Trying to flee the loading dock—he's down!"

Nash keyed his mic. "Secure him. Keep him breathing. We need him talking."

But Nickoli was nowhere. They swept the entire building—every corridor, every stairwell, every exit. No trace. Nash stepped outside into the night, the cold air biting at his face. He raised his radio again.

"This is Chief Nash," he said. "The primary target has fled. Nickoli is not on site. I repeat—Nickoli has escaped."

There was a pause on the line. Then: "Copy that."

Across the lot, paramedics loaded survivors into ambulances, their faces pale, their bodies wrapped in blankets. Dana stood in the middle of the rotation bay, sweat streaking down her face, ash smudged across her jaw. Her eyes locked with Nash's. They had won tonight. But not completely. Nickoli was gone.

Chapter 20

Maya stood by the window, hands resting against the sill, her body tense beneath the silk robe. The alley below was still. The rescue van waited, hidden in shadows beyond the hotel's camera reach. All they needed was time. Marcus checked the clock. Three minutes until the scheduled extraction. He adjusted his sleeve and kept his posture casual, but his ears were tuned to everything. Then he heard it.

Voices in the hallway. Low at first. Then hurried footsteps. The shuffle of movement beyond the door. Someone barked an order. Something had changed.

Marcus stood slowly, walked to the window beside Maya, and drew back the curtain just enough to see the alley below. The van was still there. Still waiting. But the sense of control had vanished. Something was wrong.

He didn't look at Maya when he spoke. "Time's up."

She turned, eyes wide.

Marcus stepped across the room, unplugged the heavy lamp from the nightstand, and held it out to her.

"Take it," he said quietly.

She hesitated. "What?"

"Take the lamp. When I tell you, hit me. Hard. Then go out the window. The team will pull you out."

She looked from the lamp to his face, her expression one of confusion and fear. "Why? What's happening?"

Marcus kept his voice controlled. "There's no time to explain. They are aware of the raid, and our cover is about to be blown. They need to know that I am still Logan Harper and that you escaped…again."

"But I—"she began.

He stepped closer, pressing the lamp gently into her hands. "You've done this before. Do it again. Trust me. This is how we both walk away."

She swallowed hard, gripping the base of the lamp with both hands. Her knuckles turned white.

Marcus stepped back, took a breath, and nodded. "Now."

She swung. The world flashed white. Then black.

He hit the floor with a muffled thud, the edge of the bed breaking his fall. Pain cracked across the side of his head. The ceiling swam above him.

He barely heard the window open. A gust of wet air swept into the room. Then the door burst open.

Two guards stormed in, weapons drawn. One scanned the room. "Window's open."

The other knelt beside Marcus, checking his pulse. "She hit him. Bastard didn't see it coming."

"You see where she went?" the first guard asked.

"North side alley," the second guard replied.

They bolted out of the room. Marcus let the pain wash over him. His heart pounded. Blood ran warm down his temple, pooling beneath his cheek. It worked. A minute later, the hallway filled again—this time with real officers. The guards were intercepted and tackled outside the elevator. Voices shouted. Radios crackled. Medics entered the suite. Marcus blinked as a flashlight passed across his face.

"You're okay," one of them said. "You might have a mild concussion, but you're okay."

He pushed the medic's hand away, blinking hard. "The girl? Maya?"

Someone answered from the doorway. "She made it. The extraction team confirmed. She's safe."

Marcus exhaled, the pressure in his chest finally giving way. He stared at the ceiling, the lights above too bright now.

The hotel room blurred at the edges, but he didn't care. Maya was gone. The plan had held.

Logan Harper had been attacked, but Marcus Cole was still in the game.

* * *

Back at the command center—a dimly lit, concrete room now filled with the aftershocks of chaos—Marcus stood hunched over a desk, a blood-stained bandage taped above his brow. Elaine worked silently at her laptop, fingers moving faster than the storm outside.

Dana leaned against the wall, arms crossed, eyes fixed on the surveillance feed still frozen on Suite 209. Her jaw clenched.

"She made it," Marcus said, breath tight.

Dana exhaled slowly. "Then we got one thing right tonight."

But the moment was brief. Elaine straightened suddenly, her eyes sharp with focus. "You said Maya gave a name," she said. "Marisol."

Marcus nodded. "She recognized her. Said she knew her from the survivor center."

Elaine typed a series of commands to narrow her search parameters. The screen filled with names, photos, and timestamps.

"There were a few Marisols in the older registries," she murmured. "But only one who had clearance to meet with survivors unsupervised. Volunteered for years."

She turned the screen toward them. Dana went pale. Rosa Vargas. The photo was from years ago. Rosa was thinner with darker hair, but unmistakably her.

Marcus stared at the screen. "That can't be right. Rosa—"

"Marisol Alvarez," Elaine corrected softly. "She was trafficked as a teen. She changed her name after she escaped. Reentered the system as Rosa Vargas before Isabel was born. But to survivors like Jenna and Maya? She was always Marisol."

Dana's voice was a whisper. "Jesus Christ."

They sat in silence for a long time. The implications crashed down like a wave. Nash entered from the far door, rain dripping from his coat. He took one look at their faces and quickly crossed the room.

"What is it?" he asked.

Dana pointed at the screen. "She was the leak. Rosa Vargas. She was in contact with the girls. She knew the safe house. She was Marisol."

Nash's expression didn't change, but something shifted in his stance. He turned, pulling out his phone. "I'm calling it in. She's done."

Chapter 21

The interrogation room was sterile and still, cloaked in that heavy silence unique to law enforcement buildings in the early hours of the morning. The overhead fluorescent light buzzed faintly, casting a pale circle over the steel table in the center of the room. Rosa Vargas sat at one end of it, unmoving. Her hands were folded neatly in front of her. Her gaze was fixed on nothing at all.

She hadn't asked for a lawyer. She hadn't said a word since she was brought in. Marcus entered first. Dana followed. Both detectives looked worn from the last seventy-two hours, but neither betrayed it in their posture. Dana set the recorder down and clicked it on.

Marcus pulled out the chair across from Rosa and sat, hands flat on the table. For a while, no one said anything.

Then, finally, Marcus spoke, his voice calm. "Isabel."

Rosa looked up. Just her name. That was all it took. Her eyes were rimmed red but dry. She hadn't cried since the arrest. Not during booking, not during the ride, not when she was placed under bright lights and given water she hadn't touched.

But now, at the sound of her daughter's name, she shifted. Something in her posture softened, then crumbled.

"Do you want to tell us the truth?" Marcus asked, voice steady. Not demanding. Not accusatory. An invitation.

Rosa's lips parted slowly as if words were foreign things she had forgotten how to use. "My name," she said after a beat, "is Marisol Alvarez. I changed it when Isabel was born. New name. New records. I needed to give her a life I never had."

Marcus nodded slightly, letting her continue.

"I was trafficked when I was fifteen. Escaped at nineteen. I was pregnant when I got out." She took a slow breath. "I didn't want anyone to know. Not the shelters, not the press. That name—Marisol—died a long time ago. Or I thought it had."

Dana leaned forward, arms crossed. "But you used it again. At the survivor centers. That's how Jenna and Maya knew you."

Rosa looked at her, then at the table. "It was the only name I could give them. The only one that still had meaning to those girls. I didn't want Isabel associated with that life."

Silence filled the room again. The ticking of the wall clock became louder.

"After I got out," Rosa continued, voice thin, "I spent years trying to help others. Girls like me. That's how I met Jenna. And Maya. They were so broken when they came in." Her voice cracked just a little. "But they survived. And I helped them."

Dana kept her eyes on Rosa. "Then why betray them?"

Rosa flinched as if the question was a slap. Her jaw tensed, and her fingers pressed tightly together. "Because the world betrayed me first."

Marcus leaned back, letting the silence stretch again.

"After Isabel went missing, I stopped everything," Rosa said. "I pulled away from the shelters. The girls.

The advocacy work. All of it. I focused on finding her. Or what was left of her."

Dana nodded, "And when she was found in that alley...?"

Rosa swallowed hard. "Something broke. I had survived everything. I had built a life. I had protected her. And it didn't matter. They got her anyway."

"Then the news ran the story," she continued. "They used my photo. I begged them not to, but it didn't matter. That was how they found me. The ones I had escaped from. The ones who used to own me. I got a call from a man, weeks after the funeral. He told me to stay quiet. He said if I cooperated, they'd let me live. If not…"

She trailed off, then after a moment, she continued." I thought if I just stayed quiet, it would go away. I didn't want to be Marisol anymore. I wanted to disappear again."

Marcus spoke gently. "But then Jenna called."

Rosa's lips trembled. "She was scared. She just wanted to hear a familiar voice. She didn't know who I was. Not really. Just someone who helped once."

"And she told you about the safehouse," Dana said.

Rosa gave a tiny nod. "I didn't ask. I swear. She volunteered it. Said it felt like a prison. Said she didn't trust the new guards. I told her to stay put. But after the call, I panicked. The man who called me before...he reached out again. Said that they had eyes everywhere and wanted to know where the girls were."

"And you told them," Marcus said.

Rosa pressed a hand to her chest. "I told myself it would just be a warning, that they would just tell the girls to stay quiet, like they told me. I didn't think they'd actually..." Her voice cracked fully now. "I didn't think they'd kill Jenna."

Her hands trembled now. It took all her strength to keep them folded.

"And Maya?" Dana asked, voice quieter now. "You were there. She saw you."

Rosa didn't speak for a long moment.

"I told them I'd only give them the location if I could go," she said finally.

Dana blinked. "What?"

"I told them...if I was going to betray those girls, I had to see them. One last time. Alive. Breathing. I wanted to see what Isabel never got to be. What she never had a chance to become."

Marcus stared at her, eyes heavy. "So you went with them. Maya said there was a woman in the car. That was you."

Rosa's voice dropped. "I just...watched from the back seat while they brought the girls out. Just a few seconds. That's all it took."

She paused, her fingers tightening in her lap.

"Maya looked right at me, and I saw it in her eyes. She recognized me."

She wiped under one eye, then gave a bitter smile.

Dana leaned forward. "You gave up the safe house just to—what? Watch them be taken?"

Rosa didn't answer right away. She stared at the wall across from her, voice like glass shattering.

"I wanted to feel something," she said. "To believe I still had the power to matter. To shape something. I was so tired of being helpless. Isabel was gone. The world moved on. But I didn't. I couldn't."

She dropped her head.

"If my daughter didn't get to live..." She stopped again. Then, finished. "Why should they?"

Marcus shook his head. "I'm having a hard time trying to figure out which side you're on," he said. "Your story is all over the place."

Dana rose abruptly and turned her back to the room. She faced the wall for a long moment, breathing through her nose. "You should have come to us," she said finally.

"Would you have believed me?" Rosa asked. "Would anyone have? A former trafficked mother of a murdered girl confessing she had ties to her old captors? You would have seen me as a suspect from the start."

Marcus didn't answer. Because she wasn't wrong. The recorder on the table blinked quietly. Marcus stood, walked to the device, and turned it off. He looked down at Rosa for a long time. "You're going to be processed," he said. "There won't be press. No leaks. But there will be consequences."

"I know," she whispered. "I never expected anything else."

Marcus turned and left the room. Dana lingered a moment longer, then followed. In the hallway, the air felt cooler. Nash waited just beyond the observation glass, holding a manila folder.

"Her file," he said simply. "We'll seal it. There won't be media."

Marcus took it. Inside the observation room, Elaine Monroe still watched. Her eyes glistened, but she didn't wipe them. As Nash stepped away, Elaine spoke softly, almost to herself. "So many of them," she whispered. "And we keep missing them."

Marcus said nothing. There was nothing left to say. Another chapter of the truth closed—quietly, bitterly, and far too late.

Chapter 22

Vince Russo sat shackled at the wrists, slouched in the cold metal chair like he was waiting for a cigarette and a story. But when the door opened and Marcus stepped through, Vince's posture straightened like a string had been pulled taut inside him. At first, he didn't speak. He just stared. Then, the realization landed like a punch.

"You," Vince muttered. "You son of a bitch."

Marcus shut the door quietly behind him and walked to the table without a word. Vince pushed back slightly in his seat, metal scraping concrete. The calm swagger Vince usually wore like a tailored suit was gone, replaced by disbelief and a flush of rage.

"Logan Harper," Vince said with venom. "That was you the whole time."

Marcus pulled out the chair opposite him and sat, placing a digital recorder on the table with deliberate calm. He hit the record button, the red light blinking steadily between them.

"My name is Detective Marcus Cole," he said evenly. "And you're going to tell me everything."

Vince laughed bitterly, shaking his head. "You played me. Got real close, didn't you? Took my card, drank my whiskey, walked through the club like you owned it. All that time, you were wired into this."

Marcus didn't blink. "You brought me in. You wanted me to see the front. What you didn't know is I was already behind the curtain."

Vince sneered, but the fight in his eyes slowly dimmed. He leaned back in the chair, exhaling hard through his nose. The anger simmered, but a different look began to surface—cynicism, maybe even respect. "So what now? You want names? Dates? Passwords?"

"Start with who you really work for," Marcus said. "You introduced Nickoli like he was the man in charge. But he wasn't, was he?"

Vince scoffed. "He was in charge of you. That much was true. But him? He's a middleman. A pit bull with a gold leash. Makes noise, shows teeth, but someone else does the walking."

"Who?" Marcus asked.

Vince gave a lazy, tired grin. "If I knew, I'd be dead. Hell, maybe I will be after this."

Marcus folded his arms, letting silence do the work. After a moment, Vince continued. "Nickoli answers to a name I never saw in print. Never heard in a room with more than one other person. We called him Cavaliere. Real ghost-type. European money. Russian ties. Maybe Italian. Who knows? Whoever he is, he's not local. He's above local."

Marcus filed the name away, his expression unreadable. "And the infrastructure? What cities are we talking about?"

"Half a dozen, minimum. The East Coast is just the storefront. The real movement happens elsewhere. New Orleans. Houston. Miami. You think it ends here, with the girls you found in the warehouse? That was inventory. One drop in a pipeline." Vince's words painted a grim picture of the crime syndicate's reach and the scale of their operations.

"And the politicians?" Marcus asked.

Vince chuckled again, but this time with something like sadness. "That's the best part. They're not the ones pulling strings. They're the ones holding the ladder. Have you ever tried to raid a building and found that the lease goes back to a nonprofit? You ever look into that nonprofit and see it's been funded by a city grant and then track that grant to a budget line item voted through by your good buddy Councilman Gaines?"

Vince leaned in, eyes glittering now. "You thought Gaines was a corrupt official. He's not. He's a facilitator. He clears the red tape. His boy Calloway smooths the ground. Everything stays clean on paper."

"Until girls go missing," Marcus said.

"Until girls go missing," Vince echoed. "And even then, there's someone to point at. A bad cop. A foreign buyer. A warehouse manager. Never the suit. Never the donor."

A silence hung over them. Marcus picked up the recorder, stopped it, and slipped it into his coat pocket.

"That's all you need?" Vince asked, sounding tired now.

"For now," Marcus said.

Vince shook his head slowly. "You think bringing down Nickoli is the win. It isn't. He won't talk. Even if you squeeze him, he doesn't know half of it. Not where the accounts are hidden. Not where Cavaliere lives. Hell, he might not even know Cavaliere's real name."

Marcus shook his head. "Then you tell me why you told me all this."

Vince looked at him with a strange flicker of vulnerability. "Because I'm bored. Because I liked Logan Harper. Because you're the only one who got close enough to see it from the inside." He gestured around the room. "Now I sit here. And you walk out. And none of it changes unless someone upstairs decides to burn it all down."

Marcus stood. "Then let's light the match."

He stood up and opened the door. Dana and Nash were standing just beyond the glass. He handed Dana the recorder.

"Hey," Vince called out behind him. "Logan. Or whatever the hell your name is now. If you go after them for real, you'll need to stop thinking like a cop."

Marcus didn't turn around. He stepped out into the hallway.

"He talk?" Nash asked.

Marcus nodded. "We've been playing chess with a pawn."

Dana looked at him. "Then what's the next move?"

Marcus stared through the glass at Vince, still seated, still smirking. "We find the board."

Chapter 23

Marcus stood alone in the evidence room, surrounded by shelves of dust-covered files and the dim hum of fluorescent lighting. He flipped through case file after case file, the pages whispering like ghosts in the silence. Each report, each photograph, each handwritten note added another weight to his shoulders. The deeper he looked, the clearer it became: this wasn't just a network; it was a system. It was a machine, and the rot had seeped into the gears a long time ago.

Vince's words from the interrogation echoed in his mind—cold, deliberate, undeniable. Nickoli was just a lieutenant. Not the mastermind. Not the one pulling the strings. The revelation hadn't landed like a bomb; it had settled like dust, creeping into everything. Every page Marcus touched now carried that implication. Every face in those folders looked different. Like maybe they'd all been dancing on strings, too.

He hadn't moved in nearly twenty minutes when Dana's voice cut through the silence.

"You look like hell," she said, stepping into the room with a coffee in one hand and a folder in the other.

Marcus didn't look up right away. He blinked once, as if pulling himself out of a deep tunnel, then finally took the coffee with a quiet nod. His hands were stiff as he accepted the folder.

"Thought you might want to see this," Dana added, watching him carefully.

He opened it slowly. At first, just routine logs and call traces. Nothing unusual. But a few pages in, he stopped. His eyes fixed on a cluster of timestamps, his thumb pressing against the edge of the paper. A series of calls. Richard Gaines. Darren Calloway. Multiple conversations, all within a tight three-day window, just before the warehouse raid.

"They knew it was coming," Marcus murmured.

"Or they were preparing for the fallout," Dana replied, her tone clipped but steady. "Elaine traced the line to a burner registered through one of Gaines's shell companies. That same company leases at least five buildings we've flagged as drop zones."

Marcus stared at the records a moment longer. Then, without a word, he snapped the folder shut. "We need to go deeper."

* * *

By late evening, the operations room had transformed into something that resembled a war bunker more than a precinct office. The hum of electronics filled the air, punctuated by the occasional clack of a keyboard or the shuffle of papers. Whiteboards covered in scribbled notes and connecting lines leaned against every available surface, and string maps—once the eccentric domain of conspiracy theorists—now made up the backbone of their investigation. Laptops lay open on desks, displaying spreadsheets, city records, and flagged financial transactions. Coffee cups were everywhere.

Elaine Monroe had slipped into the chaos like she'd never left it. She sat cross-legged in one of the rolling chairs, her focus absolute as her fingers danced across the keyboard. Her face was illuminated by the pale glow of her laptop screen, a permanent squint etched into her features from hours of digging through digital rot.

"There," she said suddenly, her voice slicing through the quiet murmur of the room. She leaned forward and jabbed a finger at the monitor. "Two years ago, Gaines approved a community redevelopment fund. Half a million dollars, supposedly earmarked for affordable housing on the south end."

Dana pushed away from her own laptop and walked over, coffee in hand. She leaned in to read over Elaine's shoulder. "But that's not where it went."

Elaine tapped the screen again, highlighting a different line item. "Nope. The funds were rerouted through a subcommittee and then funneled to a nonprofit called Renewal Bridge."

Dana frowned. "Never heard of it."

"You're not supposed to," Elaine said. "It's a shell. Registered under one director—Darren Calloway. The same Calloway who handed Marcus that club invite and plays middleman for Vince."

Dana's brow furrowed. "So what's Renewal Bridge supposed to be?"

Elaine clicked open a few more tabs. "According to its charter? Youth outreach, mentorship, rehabilitation programs. But the listed address? A shuttered massage parlor that was investigated twice for trafficking."

"Any charges stick?" Marcus asked, stepping away from the board.

Elaine shook her head. "Nothing. Both cases were dropped. Witnesses recanted. Paperwork vanished."

Marcus approached and took the marker from behind his ear, jotting down the new link on the board. He paused, then drew a thick red line between Gaines and Calloway. "How many more of these so-called nonprofits are we looking at?"

Elaine's fingers flew across the keys. A few seconds passed, and then she swiveled the screen toward them. "Six. Every one of them received public funds backed by Gaines' legislation. All of them trace back to various shell corps, and all of those? Ultimately linked to offshore accounts we've seen in Nickoli's network."

Dana let out a breath, long and slow. "Jesus. We thought they were just laundering money. Turns out they were laundering legitimacy."

Marcus stepped back and stared at the board. Names, arrows, and addresses branched out like the limbs of a diseased tree. Gaines. Calloway. Renewal

Bridge. A dozen city grants. Six shell corporations. And under it all, the silent trail of victims—young girls pulled into a system so polished it looked like policy.

"We need someone to talk," he said quietly. His eyes never left the board. "Someone close to Gaines."

Elaine glanced at him, then exchanged a look with Dana. No one said it out loud, but they were all thinking the same thing. If the money didn't bring him down, maybe someone inside would.

* * *

The apartment was modest—a second-floor unit in a walk-up that smelled faintly of old radiator heat and lemon cleaner. Lisa Tremayne answered the door on the second knock, her hair pulled back, face bare, and wrapped in a hoodie that looked two sizes too large. She blinked at the sight of Marcus and Dana on the threshold, suspicion already forming in the tight line of her mouth.

"What now?" she asked.

Marcus held up his badge, and Dana did the same. "Ms. Tremayne, we're not here to cause trouble. We just need to ask you a few questions. Off the record."

She snorted. "There's no such thing as 'off the record' with the police."

Still, after a pause, she stepped back and let them in. The living room was sparsely decorated but clean. Neutral colors. A single bookshelf near the window. A folded blanket draped over one side of the couch. It looked like a place someone lived in cautiously—never too comfortable, always ready to move.

Dana remained standing while Marcus took a seat in the armchair. "You worked as Councilman Gaines's legislative coordinator," Dana began. "You handled budget drafts, monitored language on amendments. We're not here to pin anything on you. We're asking if anything ever felt…off."

Lisa crossed her arms. "You mean aside from the general circus that is city politics?"

Dana gave her a small smile, but her eyes were serious. "Beyond the usual chaos."

Lisa hesitated, her gaze shifting between them. Then she walked slowly to the sofa and sat down. "There's a lot of 'don't ask' in that world. Half the job is pretending not to notice things. Bills get passed under vague language with rushed timetables. Sometimes you see millions rerouted in an afternoon, and everyone pretends it's just bureaucracy."

Marcus leaned forward. "Did you ever question one of those reroutes?"

She nodded slowly. "Once," she said. "There was this housing fund. It looked noble—redevelopment, community outreach, all the right buzzwords. But the numbers were wrong. The transfers were too quick, the shell organizations too convenient. I flagged it in a report. Nothing accusatory, just…questions."

"And?" Dana prompted.

Lisa exhaled slowly, her voice quieter now. "Two days later, Gaines called me into his office. Shut the door. Told me that if I wanted a future in this town, I'd stop chasing ghosts and start learning what loyalty meant. He said politics was about trust, not paranoia. That people who made waves tended to drown."

Marcus sat back. "And after that?"

She looked away. "After that, I stopped looking."

Marcus reached into his coat pocket and handed her a card. "If you remember anything else, or if you ever decide to make a formal statement—"

Lisa took the card but didn't look at it. "Don't hold your breath, Detective."

She rose from the couch and walked them to the door. Just before opening it, she met Marcus's eyes again.

"But for what it's worth? I hope you bury that bastard."

* * *

Back at the precinct, the operations board had become a sprawling web of lines, pins, and names. Gaines's name sat at the center, not as a mastermind but as a linchpin. His role wasn't about command. It was about the cover. He didn't pull strings—he wrapped them in government grants, in zoning approvals, in public-facing policies that masked something rotten underneath. He didn't run the machine. He kept it polished.

Calloway's photo sat just below, lines branching off to dummy corporations, fake nonprofits, property deeds. He moved the money, filtered it, packaged it, and legitimized it. And Nickoli…Nickoli was farther down. Close to the bottom. His lines didn't point to financials or paperwork. His lines pointed to people. Broken ones. Marcus stood a few feet back from the board, arms crossed, eyes tracing the connections like a man reading his own autopsy. Beside him, Dana stared, her hand resting on the edge of the table covered in files.

"We need to move on Gaines," she said finally. "We've got enough for an internal inquiry. Maybe even a quiet subpoena if we pitch it right."

Before Marcus could respond, a voice broke in from behind. "Not yet."

They turned as Nash stepped into the room. His sleeves were rolled up, his jaw unshaven, and his eyes fixed not on them, but on the network of faces and lines dominating the wall. "You push too soon," he said, voice low and even, "and they vanish. You push too late, more girls disappear."

Marcus didn't flinch. "We're not playing a timing game anymore." He turned toward Nash, meeting him head-on. "Vince cracked. He opened the door. We're already inside. All we have to do is walk it to the end."

Nash didn't argue. He stepped closer to the board, his fingers drifting toward the red string that connected Gaines to the Renewal Bridge nonprofit. His gaze lingered there, then followed it to a set of smaller names—some familiar, some newly uncovered. He nodded slowly, the gravity of the moment settling in the lines on his face.

"I'll authorize preliminary inquiries," he said. "Quiet ones. No press. No leaks. I'll handpick the officers myself."

Marcus reached into the stack of documents beside him and slid a fresh printout across the table toward Nash. "Then start here," he said. "Gaines isn't alone. These names all relate to the same accounts—city contractors, real estate brokers, and community outreach directors. They've all been feeding off the same trough."

Nash took the sheet and scanned it in silence, the fluorescent lights above catching the weariness in his expression.

"You do realize what this starts," he said eventually. "Once this breaks, we'll be under fire from the mayor's office, the DA, maybe even the Feds. This won't stay quiet for long."

Dana stepped forward, her voice steady and sharp. "Good. That means we're finally doing something right."

No one said anything after that. The silence was its own kind of agreement—weighty, tense, but unbreakable.

They weren't just chasing shadows anymore. They were turning on the lights.

Chapter 24

The townhouse sat quiet and undisturbed, nestled between two other aging brownstones on a sleepy street in East Hollow. To any passerby, it appeared as nothing more than a neglected rental—a building left behind in the slow churn of gentrification. The windows were dust-streaked, the bricks dulled by time, ivy creeping up one side like a lazy intruder. A rusted gutter hung low over the stoop, ready to drop at the next strong wind. But Marcus knew better.

He sat behind the wheel of an unmarked sedan parked across the street, the cracked windshield doing little to distort his view of the structure. Next to him, Dana scrolled through a floor plan on a city-issued tablet, the bluish glow from the screen lighting her face in the dim interior.

"Power's still running," she murmured, not looking up. "No active lease, no listed tenants for six months. But the utility bills are being paid on time, every month. Shell corp buried under three more shells. All of them trace back to Nickoli."

Marcus didn't answer immediately. His eyes were fixed on the house. He scanned the roofline, the window seams, and the seams along the doorframe. It wasn't just quiet. It was the kind of quiet that set instincts on edge. There were no flyers jammed into the gate, no peeling notices on the door. No scuff marks from a tenant's daily life. It was too still. Too preserved.

He exhaled slowly. "No sirens. No lights. No breach team. We do this softly. Plainclothes, backup two blocks out. The last thing we need is to spook whoever might still be inside."

Ten minutes later, Marcus, Dana, and two plainclothes officers moved in a staggered approach from either side of the sidewalk. No radio chatter, no drawn weapons—just quiet steps and sharpened focus. Marcus reached the door first and knelt by the lock. A few years ago, it would've taken him five minutes.

Now, with practice and purpose, he popped it open in thirty seconds. The door gave with a reluctant creak.

The first thing that struck him wasn't a smell—it was the lack of one. No mildew, no dust, no rot. Just the sharp, flat taste of processed air. Like an empty server room. Or a morgue. The entryway was pristine. A pair of women's black heels rested near the stairs, perfectly aligned. An umbrella leaned in the corner, its price tag still dangling from the handle. The living room was spotless, staged almost. Couch cushions perfectly fluffed. A single magazine on the coffee table, unopened. It looked less like a home and more like a showroom waiting for its next client.

Dana stepped beside him, voice low. "This wasn't abandoned. It was curated."

Marcus gave a tight nod, then moved further in. The kitchen was equally untouched—clean counters, shining appliances, not a single crumb or dish in sight. A drawer filled with takeout menus gave away the illusion—every one dated within the last two weeks. Someone had been living here. Or at least using it. And recently.

They split up to sweep the house. Dana took the staircase, moving quietly, pistol drawn. Marcus turned toward the rear of the kitchen, where a hallway narrowed into shadow. At the end of it, a single door stood out—not for its design, but for the wear. The paint around the knob was scuffed, the metal dulled and scratched. Someone had handled it often. He reached for it, easing it open with practiced care. A stairwell descended into darkness.

He flicked on his flashlight and descended slowly, the beam bouncing off the cement walls as the air turned cold and dry. Each step felt heavier than the last. At the bottom, the narrow basement opened into a rectangular room—bare concrete, industrial lighting overhead, and at the far wall, a single door.

He reached for his radio. "Dana," he said. "Basement. You'll want to see this."

Minutes later, she appeared behind him, eyes narrowing at the door. Together, they breached it. The room inside was chaos contained. A makeshift command center, hastily dismantled. Wires hung like veins from broken routers and shattered monitors. Metal desks had been flipped or partially scorched. A blackened trash can in the corner still smoldered faintly, the acrid stink of melted plastic clinging to the air. In the center of it all, a half-melted laptop sat on a slab of concrete, its screen fused to the keyboard.

"Jesus," Dana muttered, covering her mouth. "They torched the place. Couldn't have been more than a day or two ago."

Marcus crouched beside the wreckage, his flashlight angled just right. Despite the damage, some of the circuitry in the back casing looked untouched.

"We might be able to recover fragments," he said. "Depends on how deep the wipe went."

He turned to the next table and paused. A fireproof lockbox lay open, its contents scorched but not destroyed. Dana carefully pulled out one of the documents with gloved hands, holding it close to her light.

The pages were charred at the edges, but readable in places. Offshore banks. Routing codes. A typed note near the bottom caught her eye: "CAVALIERE – 3/7 – shipment rerouted via Milan."

She looked up slowly. "You seeing what I'm seeing?"

Marcus's jaw tensed. "Vince wasn't exaggerating. Nickoli's not the top. There's someone else. Someone higher."

They worked quickly, taking photos and securing what they could. Dana radioed for the forensics team to enter cautiously. Marcus lingered near the kitchen, walking the room one last time, when he felt it under his foot.

"Don't move," he said sharply, voice cutting through the radio.

Dana froze as Marcus dropped to a knee near the back of the kitchen island. A thin wire ran from the floor panel to a small, square device tucked beneath the counter lip—nearly invisible. He followed the casing with his fingers, locating the trigger.

"I stepped on a trip-ignition," he muttered. "Chemical-based. Low blast radius. 45 seconds on the timer. We need to go."

He keyed his mic. "We've got a device. All units back out. Evac immediately."

They cleared the building fast, shouting for forensics to fall back. Marcus and Dana had barely reached the sidewalk when the blast went off—a sharp, contained explosion that blew out the rear windows and sent a column of black smoke curling into the sky. Across the street, they watched in stunned silence, the roar still echoing in their ears.

Dana coughed, pulling her jacket over her face. "That wasn't meant to kill. That was meant to send a message."

Marcus's eyes were still on the flames, his voice low and cold. "Nickoli's not just hiding anymore. He's watching. And he wants us to know—our time's running out."

Chapter 25

The morning air inside the precinct was tense, heavy with the kind of stillness that settled before bad news or hard choices. Fluorescent lights buzzed overhead, casting a sterile glow across the briefing room's scuffed linoleum and fingerprint-smudged windows. Marcus paced slowly across the floor, a case folder clutched in one hand, the edges softening under the pressure of his grip. Each pass brought him closer to the window, then back toward the table, as if motion alone might loosen the knot twisting in his gut.

Across the room, Dana sat perched at the edge of the table, one foot planted on the floor, the other swinging idly beneath her. Her eyes tracked Marcus with that same narrowed expression she wore when chasing leads that didn't quite add up—part concern, part challenge. She brought a mug to her lips, took a sip of coffee that had probably been sitting in the pot since before sunrise, and lowered it with a quiet sigh.

"You're sure Gaines didn't see you at the gala?" she asked, her voice cutting through the silence.

Marcus paused mid-step. His eyes flicked to the frosted glass window, watching the distorted blur of movement in the hallway beyond. "We never spoke," he said at last. "I was Logan Harper. Blended in. Stayed out of his orbit."

Dana didn't look satisfied. "He was the host, Marcus. His eyes were everywhere. All it takes is one flicker of recognition, and your entire alias falls apart."

Marcus approached the table and set the folder down with more force than necessary. The papers inside shifted slightly, edges curling upward from the moisture in his palms. He let out a slow exhale and met her gaze.

"I know," he said, the weight of it plain in his tone. "But we can't sit around waiting for the perfect scenario. Vince's confession puts Gaines damn near the center of this thing. If we hesitate, he's going to bury every trail leading to him before we can take a single step."

Dana was quiet for a moment, then gave a reluctant nod. She pushed off the table, straightened her jacket, and tossed the last of the coffee into a nearby trash can. Her expression hardened, settling into resolve. "Then let's go see the gatekeeper," she said.

* * *

They didn't arrive with fanfare. No uniforms. No squad cars. Just a rented sedan with government plates and a quiet walk up to the Councilman's private office above a quiet legal building. Gaines had insisted on keeping a workspace away from City Hall, out of the public eye. That choice now played against him.

He stood when they entered, a man too seasoned to show surprise but too intelligent not to read the tension in their faces. His office was all smooth leather and mahogany paneling, framed photos of ribbon cuttings and overseas trips lining the walls. A portrait of him shaking hands with a state senator hung behind his desk, angled perfectly for press briefings.

"Well," Gaines said smoothly, gesturing toward the seats in front of him, "to what do I owe the pleasure, Detective?"

Dana took the lead. "Councilman, we're conducting an internal audit on city-funded partnerships. We need to ask you a few questions about some of your campaign donors and property acquisitions tied to housing initiatives."

Gaines didn't blink. "Of course. Though I'd appreciate some advance notice next time. Transparency is important to my office."

Marcus pulled out a printed spreadsheet. "We're specifically interested in this fund," he said, placing it on the desk. "It diverted over half a million dollars to a nonprofit that never filed a proper charter. That nonprofit owned three shell companies, all of which held leases on properties now linked to human trafficking arrests."

Gaines scanned the document with deliberate calm. "That's a serious accusation, Detective."

"It's not an accusation," Dana said flatly. "It's a question. We're hoping you can shed some light."

Gaines leaned back in his chair, steepling his fingers. "Those allocations were processed through legal channels. I don't handle the daily disbursements. I trust my aides and financial managers to vet recipients."

"And Darren Calloway?" Marcus asked. "How does he factor in?"

The Councilman's fingers twitched, a slight breath drawn through the nose. "He's...a consultant. Occasionally. I've used him for logistics, including event planning and security. He's connected, and sometimes that's what gets the job done."

"He's also connected to Vince Russo," Marcus added. "And a man by the name of Nickoli."

Gaines shifted. "I have met with a lot of people, Detective. That doesn't mean I know what they're into."

Dana slid forward. "We believe you do. We believe that your silence enabled this network to operate under the city's radar. Properties used for trafficking were rented with city funds under your signature. We're not talking about negligence. We're talking facilitation."

A long silence stretched between them. Finally, Gaines leaned forward, his voice dropping. "You don't understand how this city works. You think you're pulling a thread. You're not. You're unearthing a sewer pipe. Everyone's knee-deep in it, whether they know it or not. You go after me, it won't stop at City Hall. It'll go federal. And they won't let that happen."

"Then tell us who they are," Marcus said.

Gaines hesitated. "You think this ends with me? I'm not the architect," he said bitterly. "I tried to back out once over suspicions. Do you know what happened? My driver—he disappeared. Vanished. They made it clear I wasn't allowed to leave the table."

"Who are 'they'?" Dana asked.

Gaines stared at her, then past her. "You're chasing faces and street names. You should be chasing money. Offshore accounts. Anonymous donors. One of the major handlers is overseas. Banker type. He never touches the product, but he keeps the machine fed. All the payments go through him."

"Name," Marcus demanded.

"I don't know," Gaines said. "Goes by Cavaliere in their circles. You'll never pin him down. Diplomatic ties. International charities. But he's your vault. He's the one with the client lists."

He straightened his tie and leaned back. "So now what? You arrest me? Parade me through the courthouse?"

"We're submitting a formal request to the State's Attorney," Dana said. "Right now, this is still an inquiry. But don't mistake our restraint for leniency."

As they stood, Gaines looked at Marcus again, something probing in his eyes. "You know," he said slowly, "you look familiar."

Marcus kept his expression still. "That so?"

"Yes." Gaines tilted his head. "I can't place it, though."

Marcus gave a slight shrug. "I guess I just have one of those faces."

There was a pause. Just long enough for the silence to grow uncomfortable. Then Gaines smiled. "Well, Detective. If I think of it, I'll be sure to let you know."

* * *

Back at the precinct, Marcus sat with Nash in the office, the blinds drawn tight.

"You believe him?" Nash asked, flipping through the report.

"I believe he's scared," Marcus replied. "That makes him useful. But he's still a bastard."

Nash nodded. "Then we press forward. But this thing's going to draw blood. You're moving into territory that doesn't play by street rules. People like Gaines don't go down easily. They burn everything on the way out."

Marcus stared at the window, eyes unfocused. "Then we make sure what's left is worth rebuilding."

Nash closed the file, his expression tight. "I'll file the request with the feds. Quietly. But the more we know, the more dangerous this gets."

Outside, the city moved on, oblivious to the rot just beneath its skin. But for Marcus, there was no turning back. The political shields were falling. And whatever was left behind would finally have to answer for the lives it had buried.

Chapter 26

Elaine's laptop lit her living room like a campfire in the dark. Marcus stood nearby, sipping black coffee as he leaned on the back of a worn-out armchair. The silence between them was taut, filled with the low hum of a computer fan and the rhythmic tap of Elaine's fingers.

Elaine's eyes darted between windows on her screen, each one a puzzle piece in a complex game. "VPN routing out of Malta," she muttered, her voice a whisper in the labyrinth of data, "then doubled through Zurich before bouncing off a dead node in Jakarta. But...he slipped."

Marcus raised an eyebrow. "Who?"

Elaine didn't look away from the screen. "Cavaliere."

She hit a key. The window blinked and reorganized into a flowchart, displaying names, accounts, and timestamps. Her cursor hovered over a node tagged with a pseudonym and a string of IP logs. She clicked again, and a new screen filled with entries: wire transfers, donor logs, property leases, all tied to an alias the task force had only recently begun to understand.

"His real name is Luca de Rossi," she said, voice tight with something between triumph and disbelief.

Marcus shifted. "So we have a name for Cavaliere now?"

Elaine nodded. "Italian financier. Lives in Milan. And guess what? He holds diplomatic credentials through a consultancy role with a cultural exchange nonprofit funded by three countries."

"Let me guess," Marcus said, moving closer. "All three have convenient extradition loopholes."

"Ding ding," she said. "He's got the trifecta—money, immunity, and friends in high places."

Marcus crossed his arms. "And here I thought my job was hard. How the hell do you even find this stuff?"

Elaine turned toward him, arching an eyebrow. "Journalism is an annoyingly skilled profession,

Detective. You'd be surprised how often the truth hides in the footnotes."

Marcus grinned and took another sip of his coffee. "Have you ever considered working in intelligence?"

She rolled her eyes. "God, no. They wear too much beige and are bogged down in red tape. Besides, the pay sucks."

He gave a low chuckle, then nodded toward the screen. "Tell me everything."

Elaine turned back to the laptop. "Cavaliere—or de Rossi—has moved money through at least nine international shell companies over the past three years. The signature on these transactions matches the same encoded watermark that we found embedded in the ledgers from the townhouse."

Marcus leaned in. "The townhouse Nickoli tried to torch?"

"The very one," she confirmed. "De Rossi also donates to several 'philanthropic' organizations. Guess who else shows up on those guest lists?"

She clicked, and a new folder opened. A high-resolution image filled the screen—Councilman Richard Gaines, drink in hand, laughing at some black-tie event. Right behind him, partially obscured, stood

Darren Calloway. A few frames later, Luca de Rossi appeared, speaking with someone in a tuxedo.

Marcus exhaled sharply. "Well, well. Gaines has friends abroad."

"More than friends," Elaine said. "There's a whole transatlantic web. The shell companies through which de Rossi moves money are also listed as silent partners in three American nonprofit groups that supposedly help relocate refugees. In reality? They're laundering operations. The same groups bought property later tied to Elite Opportunities."

Marcus sat down slowly on the edge of her couch. "So he's the one holding the strings."

Elaine nodded. "Nickoli was a manager. De Rossi is the banker."

"Is he touchable?"

"Not through law enforcement," Elaine said. "Diplomatic immunity. He's technically an advisor to a UN cultural preservation body. It would take a scandal of international proportions to even get him detained, let alone charged."

"So what does that mean?" Marcus asked, rubbing his jaw.

Elaine leaned back. "It means we don't take him down with badges and warrants. We bait him with Logan Harper."

* * *

Back at the precinct, Nash listened in silence as Marcus and Elaine laid out the findings. The chief's office smelled faintly of leather and old coffee, and a soft drizzle tapped against the window, muffling the tension inside.

"Let me get this straight," Nash said, looking between the two. "This Cavaliere, or de Rossi, is the financial brain behind the trafficking network?"

"Yes," Marcus said. "And he's untouchable through conventional channels."

"And you're proposing," Nash continued, "that we revive Logan Harper and make de Rossi think he's still in play."

Elaine nodded. "We use his ego and his need to control the market. We leak that Harper survived the bust, that he's flush with untraceable cash, and that he's looking to invest in relocation infrastructure—quietly."

Nash narrowed his eyes. "That would mean giving Marcus another false identity run. More exposure."

Marcus leaned forward. "We'll fake a series of transactions through one of Cavaliere's flagged shell companies. If he's watching, and we know he is, he'll notice."

Elaine added, "And if he thinks Logan Harper is back in the game, he'll either reach out—or let Nickoli do it for him."

Nash drummed his fingers on the table. "And what makes you think Nickoli would bite?"

"Because he's desperate," Marcus said. "After the warehouse raid, after the townhouse firetrap, he's scattered. He knows he's exposed. But if he thinks Harper is still useful to Cavaliere, he won't run. He'll try to rebuild."

Silence followed. Then Nash said, "Fine. But no screwups. We do this clean. I want every burner, every movement, every asset tracked."

Marcus nodded. "We'll need to contact INTERPOL. Quietly."

Nash opened a drawer and slid out a business card. "Sergeant Ocampo, Milan division. We worked on a human smuggling case together five years ago. If anyone knows how to track de Rossi's movements, it's her."

The next morning, Elaine met Marcus in the cybercrime lab on the fourth floor of a borrowed federal building. The team had been granted temporary access through Nash's quiet strings. On-screen, Harper's name appeared in dummy accounts linked to dormant donor groups and shell companies. De Rossi's watchers would see everything—an interested buyer with resources, anonymity, and appetite.

"Tracker's in place," Elaine said. "One traceable wire transfer goes out tonight. If they're watching, it'll light up every node they've ever used."

Marcus checked the timestamp and nodded. "Then we wait."

Elaine didn't answer right away. Then she said quietly, "You sure you're ready to wear that mask again?"

He met her eyes. "We don't have a choice."

She paused. "You do. You always do."

Marcus glanced at the screen again. Logan Harper blinked in red across the network. A lie, yes—but one built to destroy a greater truth.

"No," he said. "Not anymore."

Chapter 27

Marcus hadn't worn the skin of Logan Harper in weeks, but the moment demanded it—and the man returned with unsettling ease. It started in the dark—both literally and digitally. Before the sun had even thought about rising, Marcus sat hunched at the corner desk in Elaine's downtown loft, now transformed into something between a hacker's den and a federal war room. Elaine stood behind Marcus with her arms crossed, her face framed by the pale blue light of three separate monitors.

"He's ready," she said, her voice low but certain. With a final keystroke, she uploaded a cluster of forged digital footprints—transaction histories, login records, tax echoes, and bank transfers that wove Logan Harper into the web of Cavaliere's criminal machinery. "Logan Harper now owns partial shares in two shell companies that Cavaliere used to funnel cash through Eastern Europe. One of them even paid rent on that villa outside Naples."

Marcus leaned back slightly, rubbing his jaw. "Too obvious?" he asked, though he already knew the answer.

Elaine didn't hesitate. "No. Just obvious enough to make someone nervous." She tapped a few keys, adjusting the metadata one last time. "A dead man buying old assets tends to rattle cages. It makes people look over their shoulder. It makes them wonder who's still breathing."

With a few more strokes, she queued the final piece: a post on a hidden board in the deep web, one monitored by eyes they knew would be watching. The headline was simple, almost sterile, but it carried weight like a loaded weapon:

One of Cavaliere's ghosts walks again. Client list active. Untraceable cash only.

Elaine clicked *enter*. And then they waited.

* * *

By morning, the burner phone rang. No caller ID. No traceable signal. Marcus picked it up and said nothing. The voice that answered was male. Calm. Accented but hard to place. "Are you looking for new business, Mr. Harper?"

Marcus paused just long enough. "Depends who's asking."

"You'll know soon enough," the voice replied before there was a click.

Twenty-seven minutes later, Elaine's screen lit up. A packet of encrypted coordinates was delivered through a hidden relay routed through three anonymized networks.

"Whoever that was, they didn't buy in halfway," she said. "This is custom encryption—military-grade. European black market. I'm talking serious connections."

She slid the coordinates to Nash, who had arrived ten minutes earlier with Dana in tow. Neither looked like they trusted what was happening, but they knew better than to interrupt the rhythm now. Marcus had stepped too far into the current. Pulling him out would drown them all.

Dana stood near the window, arms folded tight. "You think it's Nickoli?"

"It's someone close to him," Marcus said. "They wouldn't use this kind of network unless it was sanctioned. Cavaliere's name is like pulling a pin on a grenade. You don't throw it unless you want the explosion."

Nash scratched the stubble on his jaw. "We'll post teams at every ingress point near the drop. No radios. Line of sight only. If you get made—"

"I know," Marcus said.

"I mean it," Nash said. "If they sense anything off—anything—Logan Harper vanishes, and so do we."

Marcus nodded. "Then I better be convincing."

* * *

The meeting point was a decommissioned rail yard on the outskirts of the city—an expanse of rusted tracks and skeletal cranes where wind swallowed sound and no one looked too closely at a parked car. It was the kind of place where things went to die: trains, industries, people with secrets. Marcus arrived alone, the tires of his unmarked sedan crunching over gravel before coming to a slow, deliberate stop.

He stepped out wearing a slate-gray suit, tailored but not flashy, the kind of cut that whispered wealth without shouting. No tie. No badge. His hair was slicked back with just enough precision to echo the persona he hadn't inhabited in weeks. Logan Harper. The name fit again like a well-worn glove. He adjusted his cuffs, exhaled slowly, and moved like a man who didn't just expect danger—he welcomed it. A man who carried leverage in one pocket and a loaded bluff in the other.

There was no wire. No backup in the shadows. Just a discreet pulse sensor clipped to his belt, transmitting vitals in real time to the screens back at Elaine's loft. Dana had insisted on that. If things went south, at least they'd know when his heart stopped beating. Marcus checked his watch. 11:02. Two minutes past the scheduled time. He didn't fidget. Logan Harper didn't check over his shoulder. He waited.

Then came the sound—low, smooth, predatory. A black SUV rolled into view, tires whispering across the dirt, engine purring like a panther. No license plate. Tinted windows. It pulled to a stop twenty feet from him and sat there, humming in the silence. The doors didn't open. They wanted him to wait. Test his patience. Gauge his confidence.

Marcus stepped forward without hesitation, hands relaxed at his sides. The driver's window lowered just an inch, enough for a voice—disembodied, male, unfamiliar—to cut through the space between them. "You Harper?"

Marcus didn't blink. "Depends. You buying?"

A pause. Then the rear door clicked open. A man stepped out, dressed in dark civilian layers—tactical fabric disguised as streetwear. Everything about his posture suggested he was trained and deliberate. Marcus caught the faint outline of a weapon beneath the jacket and filed it away.

"You were dead," the man said.

Marcus gave a slight shrug, the corner of his mouth twitching with just enough arrogance to feel earned. "Rumors make money. Dead men don't collect."

The man studied him for a long moment, then jerked his chin toward the vehicle. "Get in."

Marcus climbed into the back without hesitation. The door thudded shut behind him, sealing out the cold and the night. The interior was dim, shadows layered deep across the leather seats. Opposite him sat another man, motionless, face obscured but presence unmistakable. Power clung to him like expensive cologne—subtle, inescapable. As Marcus's eyes adjusted, the figure turned. It wasn't Nickoli. Not yet.

But the moment wasn't a meeting—it was a test. An audition.

* * *

Back at the loft, Dana paced in tight circles, her hands behind her back, jaw tense. Nash stood beside the console, watching Marcus's vitals track across the screen.

"He's calm," Nash said, not looking away. "Maybe too calm."

Elaine didn't glance up. Her fingers danced across the keyboard, lines of code updating in real time. "We've got a secondary ping. Money just moved from Harper's shell account into an offshore trust tied to Cavaliere's Montenegro holdings. They saw it. They're tracing him."

Dana stopped pacing. "That means it's working."

"Or," Elaine muttered, still typing, "it means they're preparing to put a bullet in his skull and toss the body into the Adriatic."

Dana shot her a glare. "Really?"

Elaine gave a faint shrug. "Just covering all outcomes."

* * *

Inside the SUV, the man in the shadows leaned forward. A jagged scar curved from the base of his ear down past the collar of his coat. His voice was low, deliberate—every word carved from caution.

"You disappeared," he said. "Cavaliere trusted you once."

"Then he trusted the wrong people," Marcus replied. "But I kept the receipts. I'm not here to settle old debts. I'm here to build something better."

The scarred man tilted his head slightly. "You know Cavaliere's gone?"

Marcus blinked, feigning surprise. "Gone where?"

"Dead. Vanished. Drowned. Pick a version. Doesn't matter. What matters is, the throne's empty."

Marcus let the silence draw out. They were baiting him, testing what Harper knew. Seeing if he was still wired in—or obsolete.

"Then someone else wears the crown," Marcus said at last.

A thin smile played across the man's lips. "Maybe. Or maybe the kingdom fractured. Where do you fit in?"

"I've got the product," Marcus said coolly. "Access. Capital. The same toolkit Cavaliere gave me—but sharper, and pointed in a cleaner direction."

The man didn't respond immediately. He studied Marcus, then slowly reached into his coat and pulled out a black envelope, sealed and unmarked save for a barely visible stamp pressed into the flap.

He handed it over. "Use this. Tomorrow night. Same time. New coordinates. This meeting's over."

The door opened with a mechanical thud. Marcus stepped out into the cold without a word, the envelope firm in his hand. The SUV pulled away in silence, leaving only the faint scent of engine oil and danger in its wake.

* * *

He circled twice before returning to the loft, making sure he wasn't followed. When he finally stepped inside, he held the envelope out to Elaine.

She opened it with gloved fingers, unfolding the thick black card within. At the center was a symbol—an ouroboros coiled around a downward dagger, stamped in matte silver.

Elaine's eyes narrowed. "So what now?"

Marcus turned to the window. The sky was purpling with the last light of day, night creeping fast over the city skyline.

"Now," he said, "Logan Harper walks straight into the serpent's den."

Chapter 28

The invitation had been precise. Coordinates, time, a dress code so minimalist it was practically a threat: dark jacket, no phones, come alone. Logan Harper stepped from the black car outside a secluded wine bar nestled beneath a crumbling overpass. The place wasn't on any map, not under its current name. And yet, the scent of old money, fear, and privilege hung thick in the air before he even walked in.

He wore the mask well now. Logan didn't hesitate. He let the silence do the talking as he stepped through the iron-framed doors into darkness lit only by low-hanging chandeliers and wine racks stacked like coffins. The place had once been a haven for collectors

—now it was repurposed for deals too expensive for daylight.

Nickoli was already seated. He sat at a corner table draped in shadow, a half-empty glass of something red and expensive in his hand. Two men flanked him—both wiry, both alert, both armed. It wasn't a greeting so much as a statement: *we knew you were coming the second you left your car,* it echoed in his ear.

Marcus approached slowly, coat unbuttoned, palms visible. No fear. He slid into the seat opposite Nickoli and let the moment stretch until Nickoli broke it with a smile.

"Well," Nickoli said, "Logan Harper. I had my doubts—but you played it well."

Marcus returned the smile, cold and casual. "Still dressing like a man who doesn't expect to bleed."

Nickoli laughed, a short exhale through the nose. The kind of laugh that carried no genuine mirth, only control. "Still sharp. Good. You'll need that."

He leaned back, and Marcus finally got a complete look at him. He hadn't changed much. Slick gray suit, not a wrinkle out of place. His hands were perfectly manicured, the kind of detail most men overlooked, but Marcus knew what it meant—power, precision, vanity.

His eyes were darker than before. Smarter. And utterly unafraid.

"I should tell you," Nickoli said, "I knew you weren't real months ago. The moment Cavaliere's name started resurfacing, I had analysts watching every financial node that might echo his style. You? You were a ghost pretending to haunt. But I let it play out."

"Why?" Marcus asked, voice even.

"Because I wanted to see who you were working for. And more importantly, who you could flush out."

He took another sip, nodding toward one of his men. The guard set down a small black case on the table and opened it with a soft *click*.

Inside: a phone, a black keycard, and a folded sheet of paper.

"A choice," Nickoli said. "You walk away now, take the keycard, and become what Cavaliere wanted you to be. A buyer. A facilitator. No guilt. No cause. Just quiet, clean wealth. I can have your account filled by midnight."

Marcus didn't reach for the case.

Nickoli's tone dropped, softer. "You've seen what happens to people who try to burn the machine. Cops die. Witnesses vanish. Do you really think anything you're building survives?"

"I'm not building anything," Marcus said. "I'm tearing it down."

The smile vanished. For a beat, the room felt like it held its breath. Then, without looking, Nickoli gave a slight nod to his left. Suddenly, there was gunfire upstairs. Sharp, fast, and close. The sound of shattering glass, screams, and the unmistakable boom of a flashbang shook the dust loose from the ceiling. SWAT had breached.

Nickoli was on his feet instantly, the calm gone from his face. He spun toward the back, barking something in Russian to his guards. One grabbed the case, and the other reached for Marcus, but Marcus was faster. He pivoted the chair up with his leg, slammed it into the man's chest, and lunged. Elbow, throat, fist— by the time the second guard reached for his sidearm, Marcus was already moving. Nickoli was running, and Marcus surged after him.

The stairwell was steel and concrete, lit only by a dim security bulb that flickered as if undecided about surviving the evening. Marcus hit the first step hard, boots echoing. Nickoli had a head start, but Marcus had rage.

He caught up on the second landing. Nickoli turned and swung a bottle like a club. The glass shattered against Marcus's forearm, slicing through his jacket, but he powered through it. They hit the ground hard. Fists, knees, blood. The air was thick with sweat and violence. Nickoli was stronger than he looked—desperate men usually were. But Marcus had been carrying this moment since Jenna. Since Maya. Since Isabel. Every punch was a memory.

Nickoli tried to reach for a knife on his belt, but Marcus slammed his wrist against the railing and felt the bone crack. Nickoli howled. They rolled again, this time slamming into the exit door. It burst open and dumped them into an alley reeking of diesel and rot. Sirens echoed somewhere in the distance. The city was watching now. Marcus pulled the cuffs from his boot. Clicked one on and forced Nickoli's wrist behind his back.

"You think this means anything?" Nickoli spat, blood pooling in his mouth. "You'll never find the ledger."

Marcus held him by the collar, breathing hard. "You're wrong."

Nickoli's mouth curled upward despite the blood. "Then you still don't understand."

Marcus yanked him upright. "You're going to lead us to it."

The wine bar was a warzone. Dozens of people were arrested. Sub-basement rooms filled with evidence —documents, photos, a few survivors trembling behind locked doors. Dana stood near one of the trucks, helmet off, radio clipped to her vest. She was bruised but alive, eyes scanning the scene like a field general tallying the cost.

Nash approached from the far side, barking orders to a pair of agents boxing up seized electronics.

Marcus emerged from the back of a cruiser, bloodied, cuffed Nickoli in tow. The man no longer looked untouchable. He looked human. And small.

Dana's eyes locked on Marcus. "You good?"

"I will be," he said. "He's talking."

Nickoli didn't respond, just smiled quietly to himself.

Nash frowned. "About the ledger?"

"Not yet," Marcus said. "But he's nervous. And if he's nervous, it means it exists."

Elaine appeared behind them, holding a drive in one hand, gloves still on. "This was behind a false wall in the office. It's not the ledger. But it's close."

"What is it?" Dana asked.

Elaine held it up. "Transactions. Partial names. Payment routes. But all encrypted. This is Cavaliere's fingerprint."

Marcus looked back at Nickoli, who met his gaze with something like resignation—and something else. Faith. Not in salvation. But in the depths of what still remained hidden.

Chapter 29

The hum of the federal operations center was different now. Not the manic thrum of an unfolding crisis but the deep, methodical churn of something heavier, permanent. It was the sound of systems catching up to silence, of walls closing around men who had built their empires behind locked doors and false names.

Marcus stood at the center of it all, watching digital files blossom across a curved array of monitors. Elaine stood beside him, pale and exhausted but steady. The black circles beneath her eyes were badges earned through long nights and short sleep, but her hands were sure as she paged through printouts and cross-referenced open files.

"There's no master document," she said, eyes never leaving the screens. "But the fragments align. Encrypted logs from the townhouse. Ledger spreadsheets from Russo's club. Nickoli's backup drives. They weren't careful with their records because they didn't think anyone would get close enough to see them all at once."

Marcus nodded faintly. "And now?"

"Now they're bleeding," she said. "And we're still sharpening the knife."

They stood in silence for a long moment, the light from the monitors casting pale reflections off the steel and glass around them. Far off in another room, the quiet rumble of voices rose and fell—agents, translators, and analysts pushing every name and dollar across jurisdictional borders like chess pieces.

Elaine pulled up another window. "Interpol has initiated asset freezes tied to Cavaliere's holding companies in Switzerland and Montenegro. A yacht registered under a false identity has been seized in Malta. A private art fund in Vienna is under audit. You were right about Cavaliere's fingerprints. They're all over the infrastructure, even if no one's ever seen his face."

"He's still out there," Marcus said flatly. "But his kingdom's falling apart under him."

Elaine tapped a key. "And Nickoli?"

"Hasn't said a word. Not since the arrest. Not since he smiled in the alley like he'd already made peace with his own mythology."

"He thinks silence will protect him," Elaine said.

Marcus's voice didn't waver. "It won't."

As Elaine turned to leave, Marcus gently placed a hand on her shoulder. "Are you sure you don't want to come work for us?" he asked. "You put in a lot of work and showed you have the skills."

Elaine gave a small smile, the kind that didn't quite reach her eyes. "I'm sure, Marcus."

She paused, her gaze lingering on the evidence board for a moment longer. "You enforce the law," she said quietly. "I expose the cracks in it. The moment I carry a badge, I lose the freedom to ask the questions no one wants answered. I'd rather stay on the outside—so I can keep pulling the truth into the light." Then she turned and walked out.

* * *

Vince Russo didn't need much encouragement. He flipped on the second day. His lawyer negotiated the outlines of a deal, which included a reduced sentence, minimum security, and some protection if the Bureau believed he was in danger. Vince didn't try to defend himself. He wasn't stupid. What he wanted was distance.

He gave names. Dates. Phrases. The preferred language of the buyers. The location of offshore meetings. He confirmed what they'd suspected about Councilman Gaines and Darren Calloway—that they weren't just dirty, they were facilitators. Trusted figures who helped launder legitimacy over the entire operation. The kind of men who never stepped foot into the rooms where girls were held, but signed the contracts that kept those rooms full.

Before leaving the interrogation room, Vince dropped a final, quieter truth. "Isabel was never supposed to die," he said.

Marcus stared at him, trying to figure out if he should reply or not.

"She was taken out of rotation for retraining," Vince continued. "She fought against it. The guy handling her panicked. Dumped her body in some alley. That wasn't protocol."

Marcus shook his head. Protocol. The word sat in the air like poison. He stared at Vince, the room several degrees colder. His jaw tightened, but he said nothing. He didn't want to give the man the satisfaction of seeing him angry. He simply stood and walked out.

* * *

The next day, Councilman Richard Gaines resigned. There was no press conference. No explanation. Just a prepared statement issued through a junior aide, citing "stress-related medical concerns." Darren Calloway disappeared two hours later; his apartment was found to be empty, and his phone had been wiped clean.

Marcus returned to Rudy's Diner. The sign still flickered. The same rain had stained the sidewalk, though it was now lighter. The alley out back was clear. Just pavement and dumpsters. He stepped inside and paused for a moment, allowing his eyes to adjust to the dim, yellow glow. Rudy greeted him without words and slid an envelope across the counter.

"A new employee found this in Isabel's locker," he said. "I must have missed it before."

Marcus took the envelope and opened it. Inside was a postcard. A photo of a beach, somewhere distant and sunlit. On the back, a note in neat handwriting: *"Someday. After I make it."*

Marcus stood still for a long moment. Then he folded the card and tucked it into the pocket inside his coat. His boots left faint, wet prints behind him as he moved to the corner booth where Dana and Nash were already seated. Dana had her jacket slung over the seat beside her, a beer halfway to her lips. Nash sat stiff-backed, his coat still on, the way he always wore it in public spaces—as if he never truly let himself get comfortable. Marcus slid into the booth next to Dana as Nash reached for the pitcher in the center of the table and filled a glass. He slid it across to Marcus without looking up.

"Press is already chewing through it," he said. "Gaines out. Russo's deal on the table. We're suddenly heroes."

Dana didn't laugh, but there was the shadow of a smile behind her glass. "They call it a win when they don't know what was lost."

"They'll never know," Marcus said, wrapping his hands around the cold pint glass. "Not really."

"Some of them don't want to," Nash added.

"He's bleeding," Dana said, tipping her beer forward as if to toast it. "Cavaliere. They seized one of his properties in Tuscany. Word is the asset pool alone might trigger tax investigations in half of Europe."

"He'll vanish," Nash muttered. "People like him always do. But not unscathed."

"He's not invincible anymore," Marcus said. "That's the difference."

The silence that followed was quieter than before. It wasn't heavy. Just full.

Nash reached into his coat and pulled out an envelope, placing it on the table. "Final briefing packet. SWAT tapes, warehouse records, and hotel witness interviews. Everything wrapped. They're building a unit. Multi-agency. They want this to continue."

"They should," Dana said without hesitation. "Because it's not over."

Marcus met her eyes. "You in?"

She gave a half-smile. "You have to ask?"

Nash turned to Marcus. "And you?"

"I'm not done," Marcus said. "Not while people like Cavaliere still have places to hide."

Nash raised his glass first. "To Isabel Vargas."

Dana lifted hers. "To the ones we couldn't save."

Marcus picked up his last, staring into the amber depths as though they held something sacred. "And the ones we still can," he said.

The story that began in the alley behind Rudy's Diner had come full circle—not to peace, but to *reckoning*. Marcus Cole wasn't chasing shadows anymore. He was hunting them.

About the author:

Adam McKim was born and raised in a small town in Missouri, where he still lives today with his wife and son. He began writing in his early twenties and has authored a growing collection of poems and books. When he's not writing, he enjoys quiet moments with family and the continued pursuit of storytelling.